GOD IS AN IRON AND OTHER STORIES

GOD IS AN IRON AND OTHER STORIES

Spider Robinson

Five Star • Waterville, Maine

Five Star First Edition Science Fiction and Fantasy Series.

Published in 2002 in conjunction with Tekno-Books and Ed Gorman.

Set in 11 pt. Plantin.

Printed in the United States on permanent paper.

Library of Congress Cataloging-in-Publication Data

Robinson, Spider
      God is an iron and other stories / Spider Robinson.
         p. cm. (Five Star first edition science fiction and fantasy)
      Contents: Stardance—Melancholy elephants—God is an iron—Soul search—Local champ—Orphans of Eden—Not fade away—In the olden days—Rubber soul—The magnificent conspiracy.
      ISBN 0-7862-4162-4 (hc : alk. paper)
      1. Science fiction, American.
   PS3568.03156 G63 2002
   813'.54—dc21   2002016180

TABLE OF CONTENTS

STARDANCE
(Written with Jeanne Robinson)

I can't really say that I knew her, certainly not the way Seroff knew Isadora. All I know of her childhood and adolescence are the anecdotes she chanced to relate in my hearing—just enough to make me certain that all three of the contradictory biographies on the current best-seller list are fictional. All I know of her adult life are the hours she spent in my presence and on my monitors—more than enough to tell me that every newspaper account I've seen is fictional. Carrington probably believed he knew her better than I, and in a limited sense he was correct—but he would never have written of it, and now he is dead.

But I was her video man, since the days when you touched the camera with your hands, and I knew her backstage: a type of relationship like no other on Earth or off it. I don't believe it can be described to anyone not of the profession—you might think of it as somewhere between co-workers and combat buddies. I was with her the day she came to Skyfac, terrified and determined, to stake her life upon a dream. I watched her work and worked with her for that whole two months, through endless rehearsals, and I have saved every tape and they are not for sale.

And, of course, I saw the Stardance. I was there; I taped it. I guess I can tell you some things about her.

7

To begin with, it was not, as Cahill's *Shara* and Von Derski's *Dance Unbound: The Creation of New Modern* suggest, a lifelong fascination with space and space travel that led her to become the race's first zero-gravity dancer. Space was a means to her, not an end, and its vast empty immensity scared her at first. Nor was it, as Melberg's hardcover tabloid *The Real Shara Drummond* claims, because she lacked the talent to make it as a dancer on Earth. If you think free-fall dancing is easier than conventional dance, you try it. Don't forget your dropsickness bag.

But there is a grain of truth in Melberg's slander, as there is in all the best slanders. She could *not* make it on Earth—but not through lack of talent.

I first saw her in Toronto in July of 1984. I headed Toronto Dance Theater's video department at that time, and I hated every minute of it. I hated everything in those days. The schedule that day called for spending the entire afternoon taping students, a waste of time and tape which I hated more than anything except the phone company. I hadn't seen the year's new crop yet and was not eager to. I love to watch dance done well—the efforts of a tyro are usually as pleasing to me as a first-year violin student in the next apartment is to you.

My leg was bothering me even more than usual as I walked into the studio. Norrey saw my face and left a group of young hopefuls to come over. "Charlie . . ."

"I know, I know. 'They're tender fledglings, Charlie, with egos as fragile as an Easter egg in December. Don't bite them, Charlie. Don't even bark at them if you can help it, Charlie.' "

She smiled. "Something like that. Leg?"

"Leg."

Norrey Drummond is a dancer who gets away with looking like a woman because she's small. There's about a hundred and fifteen pounds of her, and most of it is heart. She stands about five-four, and is perfectly capable of seeming to tower over the tallest student. She has more energy than the North American Grid and uses it as efficiently as a vane pump. (Have you ever studied the principle of a standard piston-type pump? Go look up the principle of a vane pump. I wonder what the original conception of *that* notion must have been like, as an emotional experience.) There's a signature-like uniqueness to her dance, the only reason I can see why she got so few of the really juicy parts in company productions until modern gave way to new modern. I liked her because she didn't pity me.

"It's not only the leg," I admitted. "I hate to see the tender fledglings butcher your choreography."

"Then you needn't worry. The piece you're taping today is by . . . one of the students."

"Oh, fine. I knew I should have called in sick." She made a face. "What's the catch?"

"Eh?"

"Why did the funny thing happen to your voice just as you got to 'one of the students'?"

She blushed. "Damn it, she's my sister."

My eyebrows rose. "She must be good then."

"Why, thank you, Charlie."

"Bullshit. I give compliments right-handed or not at all—I'm not talking about heredity. I mean that you're so hopelessly ethical you'd bend over backward to avoid nepotism. For you to give your own sister a feature like that, she must be *terrific.*"

"Charlie, she is," Norrey said simply.

"We'll see. What's her name?"

"Shara." Norrey pointed her out, and I understood the

9

rest of the catch. Shara Drummond was ten years younger than her sister—and seven inches taller, with thirty or forty more pounds. I noted absently that she was stunningly beautiful, but it didn't deter my dismay. In her best years, Sophia Loren could never have become a modern dancer. Where Norrey was small, Shara was big; and where Norrey was big, Shara was bigger. If I'd seen her on the street I might have whistled appreciatively—but in the studio I frowned.

"My God, Norrey, she's enormous."

"Mother's second husband was a football player," she said mournfully. "She's awfully good."

"If she *is* good, that *is* awful. Poor girl. Well, what do you want me to do?"

"What makes you think I want you to do anything?"

"You're still standing here."

"Oh. I guess I am. Well . . . have lunch with us, Charlie?"

"Why?" I knew perfectly well why, but I expected a polite lie.

Not from Norrey Drummond. "Because you two have something in common, I think."

I paid her honesty the compliment of not wincing. "I suppose we do."

"Then you will?"

"Right after the session."

She twinkled and was gone. In a remarkably short time she had organized the studio full of wandering, chattering young people into something that resembled a dance ensemble if you squinted. They warmed up during the twenty minutes it took me to set up and check out my equipment. I positioned one camera in front of them, one behind, and kept one in my hands for walk-around close-up work. I never triggered it.

There's a game you play in your mind. Every time someone catches or is brought to your attention, you begin making guesses about them. You try to extrapolate their character and habits from their appearance. Him? Surly, disorganized—leaves the cap off the toothpaste and drinks boilermakers. Her? Art student type, probably uses a diaphragm and writes letters in a stylized calligraphy of her own invention. Them? They look like schoolteachers from Miami, probably here to see what snow looks like, attend a convention. Sometimes I come pretty close. I don't know how I type-cast Shara Drummond, in those first twenty minutes. The moment she began to dance, all preconceptions left my mind. She became something elemental, something unknowable, a living bridge between our world and the one the Muses live in.

I know, on an intellectual and academic level, all there is to know about dance, and I could not categorize or classify or even really comprehend the dance she danced that afternoon. I saw it, I even appreciated it, but I was not equipped to understand it. My camera dangled from the end of my arm, next to my jaw. Dancers speak of their "center," the place their motion centers around, often quite near the physical center of gravity. You strive to "dance from your center" and the "contraction-and-release" idea which underlies much of modern dance depends on the center for its focus of energy. Shara's center seemed to move about the room under its own power, trailing limbs that attached to it by choice rather than necessity. What's the word for the outermost part of the sun, the part that still shows in an eclipse? Corona? That's what her limbs were: four lengthy tongues of flame that followed the center in its eccentric, whirling orbit, writhing fluidly around its surface. That the lower two frequently contacted the floor seemed coincidental—indeed the other two touched the floor nearly as regularly.

There were other students dancing. I know this because

the two automatic videocameras, unlike me, did their job and recorded the piece as a whole. It was called *Birthing* and depicted the formation of a galaxy that ended up resembling Andromeda. It was only vaguely accurate, literally, but it wasn't intended to be. Symbolically, it felt like the birth of a galaxy.

In retrospect. At the time I was aware only of the galaxy's heart: Shara. Students occluded her from time to time, and I simply never noticed. It hurt to watch her.

If you know anything about dance, this must all sound horrid to you. A dance about a *nebula?* I know, I know. It's a ridiculous notion. And it worked. In the most gut-level, cellular way it worked—save only that Shara was too good for those around her. She did not belong in that eager crew of awkward half-trained apprentices. It was like listening to the late Stephen Wonder trying to work with a pick-up band in a Montreal bar.

But that wasn't what hurt.

Le Maintenant was shabby, but the food was good and the house brand of grass was excellent. Show a Diners Club card in there and they'd show you a galley full of dirty dishes. It's gone now. Norrey and Shara declined a toke, but in my line of work it helps. Besides, I needed a few hits. How to tell a lovely lady her dearest dream is hopeless?

I didn't need to ask Shara to know that her dearest dream was to dance. More: to dance professionally. I have often speculated on the motives of the professional artist. Some seek the narcissistic assurance that others will actually pay cash to watch or hear them. Some are so incompetent or disorganized that they can support themselves in no other way. Some have a message which they feel needs expressing. I suppose most artists combine elements of all three. This is no complaint—what they do for us is necessary. We should be grateful that there *are* motives.

But Shara was one of the rare ones. She danced because she needed to. She needed to say things which could be said in no other way, and she needed to take her meaning and her living from the saying of them. Anything else would have demeaned and devalued the essential statement of her dance. I knew this, from watching that one dance.

Between toking up and keeping my mouth full and then toking again (a mild amount to offset the slight down that eating brings), it was over half an hour before I was required to say anything beyond an occasional grunted response to the luncheon chatter of the ladies. As the coffee arrived, Shara looked me square in the eye and said, "Do you talk, Charlie?"

She was Norrey's sister, all right.

"Only inanities."

"No such thing. Inane people, maybe."

"Do you enjoy dancing, Miss Drummond?"

She answered seriously. "Define 'enjoy.' "

I opened my mouth and closed it, perhaps three times. You try it.

"And for God's sake tell me why you're so intent on not talking to me. You've got me worried."

"Shara!" Norrey looked dismayed.

"Hush. I want to know."

I took a crack at it. "Shara, before he died I had the privilege of meeting Bertram Ross. I had just seen him dance. A producer who knew and liked me took me backstage, the way you take a kid to see Santa Claus. I had expected him to look even older offstage, at rest. He looked younger, as if that incredible motion of his was barely in check. He talked to me. After a while I stopped opening my mouth, because nothing ever came out."

13

She waited, expecting more. Only gradually did she comprehend the compliment and its dimension. I had assumed it would be obvious. Most artists *expect* to be complimented. When she did twig, she did not blush or simper. She did not cock her head and say, "Oh, come on." She did not say, "You flatter me." She did not look away.

She nodded slowly and said, "Thank you, Charlie. That's worth a lot more than idle chatter." There was a suggestion of sadness in her smile, as if we shared a bitter joke.

"You're welcome."

"For heaven's sake, Norrey, what are you looking so upset about?"

The cat now had Norrey's tongue.

"She's disappointed in me," I said. "I said the wrong thing."

"That was the wrong thing?"

"It should have been 'Miss Drummond, I think you ought to give up dancing.' "

"It should have been '*Shara*, I think you ought' . . . *what?*"

"Charlie," Norrey began.

"I was supposed to tell you that we can't all be professional dancers, that they also surf who only sand and wade. Shara, I was supposed to tell you to dump the dance—before it dumps you."

In my need to be honest with her, I had been more brutal than was necessary, I thought. I was to learn that bluntness never dismayed Shara. She demanded it.

"Why you?" was all she said.

"We're inhabiting the same vessel, you and I. We've both got an itch that our bodies just won't let us scratch."

Her eyes softened. "What's your itch?"

"The same as yours."

"Eh?"

14

"The man was supposed to come and fix the phone on Thursday. My roommate Karen and I had an all-day rehearsal. We left a note. Mr. telephone man, we had to go out, and we sure couldn't call you, heh heh. Please get the key from the concierge and come on in; the phone's in the bedroom. The phone man never showed up. They never do." My hands seemed to be shaking. "We came home up the back stairs from the alley. The phone was still dead, but I never thought to take down the note on the front door. I got sick the next morning. Cramps. Vomiting. Karen and I were just friends, but she stayed home to take care of me. I suppose on a Friday night the note seemed even more plausible. He slipped the lock with a piece of plastic, and Karen came out of the kitchen as he was unplugging the stereo. He was so indignant he shot her. Twice. The noise scared him; by the time I got there he was halfway out the door. He just had time to put a slug through my hip joint, and then he was gone. They never got him. They never even came to fix the phone." My hands were under control now. "Karen was a damned good dancer, but I was better. In my head, I still am."

Her eyes were round. "You're not Charlie . . . Charles *Armstead*."

I nodded.

"Oh my God. So *that's* where you went."

I was shocked by how she looked. It brought me back from the cold and windy border of self-pity. I began a little to pity her. I should have guessed the depth of her empathy. And in the way that really mattered, we were too damned alike—we *did* share the same bitter joke. I wondered why I had wanted to shock her.

"They couldn't repair the joint?" she asked softly.

"I can walk splendidly. Given a strong enough motivation, I can even run short distances. I can't dance worth a damn."

15

"So you became a video man."

"Three years ago. People who know both video and dance are about as common as garter belts these days. Oh, they've been taping dance since the Seventies—with the imagination of a network news cameraman. If you film a stage play with two cameras in the orchestra pit, is it a movie?"

"You do for dance what the movie camera did for drama?"

"Pretty fair analogy. Where it breaks down is that dance is more analogous to music than to drama. You can't stop and start it, or go back and retake a scene that didn't go in the can right, or reverse the chronology to get a tidy shooting schedule. The event happens and you record it. What I am is what the record industry pays top dollar for—a mixman with savvy enough to know which ax is wailing at the moment and mike it high—and the sense to have given the heaviest dudes the best mikes. There are a few others like me. I'm the best."

She took it the way she had the compliment to herself—at face value. Usually when I say things like that, I don't give a damn what reaction I get, or I'm being salty and hoping for outrage. But I was pleased at her acceptance, pleased enough to bother me. A faint irritation made me go brutal again, *knowing* it wouldn't work. "So what all this leads to is that Norrey was hoping I'd suggest some similar form of sublimation for you. Because I'll make it in dance before you will."

She stubborned up. "I don't buy that, Charlie. I know what you're talking about. I'm not a fool, but I think I can beat it."

"Sure you will. *You're too damned big, lady.* You've got tits like both halves of a prize honeydew melon and an ass that any actress in Hollywood would sell her parents for, and in modern dance that makes you d-e-d dead; you haven't got a chance. Beat it? You'll beat your head in first. How'm I doing, Norrey?"

"For Christ's sake, Charlie!"

I softened. I can't work Norrey into a tantrum—I like her too much. "I'm sorry, hon. My leg's giving me the mischief, and I'm stinkin' mad. She *ought* to make it—and she won't. She's your sister, and so it saddens you. Well, I'm a total stranger, and it enrages me."

"How do you think it makes me feel?" Shara blazed, startling us both. I hadn't known she had so much voice. "So you want me to pack it in and rent me a camera, huh, Charlie? Or maybe sell apples outside the studio?" A ripple ran up her jaw. "Well, I will be damned by all the gods in Southern California before I'll pack it in. God gave me the large economy size, but there is not a surplus pound on it and it fits me like a glove and I can by Jesus *dance* it and I will. You may be right—I may beat my head in first. But I will get it done." She took a deep breath. "Now I thank you for your kind intentions, Char—Mr. Armst—Oh shit." The tears came and she left hastily, spilling a quarter-cup of cold coffee on Norrey's lap.

"Charlie," Norrey said through clenched teeth, "why do I like you so much?"

"Dancers are dumb." I gave her my handkerchief.

"Oh." She patted at her lap awhile. "How come you like me?"

"Video men are smart."

"Oh."

I spent the afternoon in my apartment reviewing the footage I'd shot that morning, and the more I watched, the madder I got.

Dance requires intense motivation at an extraordinarily early age—a blind devotion, a gamble on the as-yet-unrealized potentials of heredity and nutrition. You can begin, say, classical ballet training at age six—and at fourteen find yourself broad-shouldered, the years of total effort utterly wasted. Shara had set her sights on modern dance—and found out too late that God had dealt her the body of a woman.

She was not fat—you have seen her. She was tall, big-boned tall, and on that great frame was built a rich, ripely female body. As I ran and reran the tapes of *Birthing*, the pain grew in me until I even forgot the ever-present aching of my own leg. It was like watching a supremely gifted basketball player who stood four feet tall.

To make it in modern dance, it is essential to get into a company. You cannot be seen unless you are visible. Norrey had told me, on the walk back to the studio, of Shara's efforts to get into a company—and I could have predicted nearly every word.

"Merce *Cunningham* saw her dance, Charlie. Martha Graham saw her dance, just before she died. Both of them praised her warmly, for her choreography as much as for her technique. Neither offered her a position. I'm not even sure I blame them—I can sort of understand."

Norrey could understand all right. It was her own defect magnified a hundredfold: uniqueness. A company member must be capable of excellent solo work—but she must also be able to blend into group effort, in ensemble work. Shara's very uniqueness made her virtually useless as a company member. She could not help but draw the eye.

And once drawn, the male eye at least would never leave. Modern dancers must sometimes work nude these days, and it is therefore meet that they have the body of a fourteen-year-old boy. We may have ladies dancing with few or no clothes on up here, but by God it is Art. An actress or a musician or a singer or a painter may be lushly endowed, deli-

18

ciously rounded—but a dancer must be nearly as sexless as a high-fashion model. Perhaps God knows why. Shara could not have purged her dance of her sexuality even if she had been interested in trying, and as I watched her dance on my monitor and in my mind's eye, I knew she was not.

Why did her genius have to lie in the only occupation besides model and nun in which sexiness is a liability? It broke my heart, by empathic analogy.

"It's no good at all, is it?"

I whirled and barked, "Damn it, you made me bite my tongue."

"I'm sorry." She came from the doorway into my living room. "Norrey told me how to find the place. The door was ajar."

"I forgot to shut it when I came home."

"You leave it open?"

"I've learned the lesson of history. No junkie, no matter how strung out he is, will enter an apartment with the door ajar and the radio on. Obviously there's someone home. And you're right, it's no damn good at all. Sit down."

She sat on the couch. Her hair was down now, and I liked it better that way. I shut off the monitor and popped the tape, tossing it on a shelf.

"I came to apologize. I shouldn't have blown up at you at lunch. You were trying to help me."

"You had it coming. I imagine by now you've built up quite a head of steam."

"Five years' worth. I figured I'd start in the States instead of Canada. Go farther faster. Now I'm back in Toronto and I don't think I'm going to make it here either. You're right, Mr. Armstead—I'm too damned big. Amazons don't dance."

"It's still Charlie. Listen, something I want to ask you.

That last gesture, at the end of *Birthing*—what was that? I thought it was a beckoning; Norrey says it was a farewell; and now that I've run the tape it looks like a yearning, a reaching out."

"Then it worked."

"Pardon?"

"It seemed to me that the birth of a galaxy called for all three. They're so close together in spirit it seemed silly to give each a separate movement."

"Mmm." Worse and worse. Suppose Einstein had aphasia. "Why couldn't you have been a rotten dancer? That'd just be irony. This"—I pointed to the tape—"is high tragedy."

"Aren't you going to tell me I can still dance for myself?"

"No. For you that'd be worse than not dancing at all."

"My God, you're perceptive. Or am I that easy to read?"

I shrugged.

"Oh Charlie," she burst out, "what am I going to do?"

"You'd better not ask me that." My voice sounded funny.

"Why not?"

"Because I'm already two-thirds in love with you. And because you're not in love with me and never will be. And so that is the sort of question you shouldn't ask me."

It jolted her a little, but she recovered quickly. Her eyes softened, and she shook her head slowly. "You even know why I'm not, don't you?"

"And why you won't be."

I was terribly afraid she was going to say, "Charlie, I'm sorry." But she surprised me again. What she said was "I can count on the fingers of one foot the number of grown-up men I've ever met. I'm grateful for you. I guess ironic tragedies come in pairs."

"Sometimes."

"Well, now all I have to do is figure out what to do with my life. That should kill the weekend."

"Will you continue your classes?"

"Might as well. It's never a waste of time to study. Norrey's teaching me things."

All of a sudden my mind started to percolate. Man is a rational animal, right? Right? "What if I had a better idea?"

"If you've got another idea, it's better. Speak."

"Do you have to have an audience? I mean, does it have to be *live?*"

"What do you mean?"

"Maybe there's a back way in. Home video machines are starting to sell—once people understood they could collect old movies and such like they do records, it was just a matter of making it cheap enough for the traffic to bear. It's just about there—you know, TDT's already thinking of entering the market, and the Graham company has."

"So?"

"So suppose we go freelance? You and me? You dance it and I'll tape it: a straight business deal. I've got a few connections, and maybe I can get more. I could name you ten acts in the music business right now that never go on tour—just record and record. Why don't you bypass the structure of the dance companies and take a chance on the public? Maybe word of mouth could . . ."

Her face was beginning to light up like a jack-o'-lantern. "Charlie, do you think it could work? Do you really think so?"

"I don't think it has a snowball's chance." I crossed the room, opened up the beer fridge, took out the snowball I keep there in the summer, and tossed it at her. She caught it, but just barely, and when she realized what it was, she burst out laughing. "I've got just enough faith in the idea to quit working for TDT and put my time into it. I'll invest my time, my tape, my equipment, and my savings. Ante up."

She tried to get sober, but the snowball froze her fingers and she broke up again. "A snowball in July. You madman. Count me in. I've got a little money saved. And . . . and I guess I don't have much choice, do I?"

"I guess not."

The next three years were some of the most exciting years of my life, of both our lives. While I watched and taped, Shara transformed herself from a potentially great dancer into something truly awesome. She did something I'm not sure I can explain.

She became dance's analogy of the jazzman.

Dance was, for Shara, self-expression, pure and simple, first, last, and always. Once she freed herself of the attempt to fit into the world of company dance, she came to regard choreography, per se, as an *obstacle* to her self-expression, as a preprogrammed rut, inexorable as a script and as limiting. And so she devalued it.

A jazzman may blow *Night in Tunisia* for a dozen consecutive nights, and each evening will be a different experience, as he interprets and reinterprets the melody according to his mood of the moment. Total unity of artist and his art: spontaneous creation. The melodic starting point distinguishes the result from pure anarchy.

In just this way Shara devalued preperformance choreography to a starting point, a framework on which to build whatever the moment demanded, and then jammed around it. She learned in those three busy years to dismantle the interface between herself and her dance. Dancers have always tended to sneer at improv dancing, even while they practiced it in the studio, for the looseness it gave. They failed to see that *planned* improv, improv around a theme fully thought

22

out in advance, was the natural next step in dance. Shara took the step. You must be very, very good to get away with that much freedom. She was good enough.

There's no point in detailing our professional fortunes over those three years. We worked hard, we made some magnificent tapes, and we couldn't sell them for paperweights. A home video cassette industry indeed formed—and they knew as much about modern dance as the record industry knew about the blues when *they* started. The big outfits wanted credentials, and the little outfits wanted cheap talent. Finally we even got desperate enough to try the schlock houses—and learned what we already knew. They didn't have the distribution, the prestige, or the technical specs for the critics to pay any attention to them. Word-of-mouth advertising is like a gene pool—if it isn't a certain minimum size to start with, it doesn't get anywhere. "Spider" John Koerner is an incredibly talented musician and songwriter who has been making and selling his own records since 1972. How many of you have ever heard of him?

In May of 1987 I opened my mailbox in the lobby and found the letter from VisuEnt, Inc., terminating our option with deepest sorrow and no severance. I went straight over to Shara's apartment, and my leg felt like the bone marrow had been replaced with thermite and ignited. It was a very long walk.

She was working on *Weight Is a Verb* when I got there. Converting her big living room into a studio had cost time, energy, skull-sweat, and a fat bribe to the landlord, but it was cheaper than renting time in a studio, considering the sets we wanted. It looked like high mountain country that day, and I hung my hat on a fake alder when I entered.

She flashed me a smile and kept moving, building up to greater and greater leaps. She looked like the most beautiful mountain goat I ever saw. I was in a foul mood and I wanted to kill the music (McLaughlin and Miles together, leaping some themselves), but I never could interrupt Shara when she was dancing. She built it gradually, with directional counterpoint, until she seemed to hurl herself into the air, stay there until she was damned good and ready, and then hurl herself down again. Sometimes she rolled when she hit and sometimes she landed on her hands, and always the energy of falling was transmuted into something instead of being absorbed. It was total energy output, and by the time she was done I had calmed down enough to be almost philosophical about our mutual professional ruin.

She ended up collapsed in upon herself, head bowed, exquisitely humbled in her attempt to defy gravity. I couldn't help applauding. It felt corny, but I couldn't help it.

"Thank you, Charlie."

"I'll be damned. Weight *is* a verb. I thought you were crazy when you told me the title."

"It's one of the strongest verbs in dance—and you can make it do *anything*."

"Almost anything."

"Eh?"

"VisuEnt gave us our contract back."

"Oh." Nothing showed in her eyes, but I knew what was behind them. "Well, who's next on the list?"

"There is no one left on the list."

"*Oh.*" This time it showed. "Oh."

"We should have remembered. Great artists are never honored in their own lifetime. What we ought to do is drop dead—then we'd be all set."

In my way I was trying to be strong for her, and she knew it and tried to be strong for me.

"Maybe what we should do is go into death insurance, for

24

artists," she said. "We pay the client premiums against a controlling interest in his estate, and we insure that he'll die."

"We can't lose. And if he becomes famous in his lifetime he can buy out."

"Terrific. Let's stop this before I laugh myself to death."

"Yeah."

She was silent for a long time. My own mind was racing efficiently, but the transmission seemed to be blown—it wouldn't *go* anywhere. Finally she got up and turned off the music machine, which had been whining softly ever since the tape ended. It made a loud *click.*

"Norrey's got some land on Prince Edward Island," she said, not meeting my eyes. "There's a house."

I tried to head her off with the punchline from the old joke about the kid shoveling out the elephant cage in the circus whose father offers to take him back and set him up with a decent job. "What? And leave show business?"

"Screw show business," she said softly. "If I went out to PEI now, maybe I could get the land cleared and plowed in time to get a garden in." Her expression changed. "How about you?"

"Me? I'll be okay. TDT asked me to come back."

"That was six months ago."

"They asked again. Last week."

"And you said no. Moron."

"Maybe so, maybe so."

"The whole damn thing was a waste of time. All that time. All that energy. All that work. I might as well have been farming in PEI—by now the soil'd be starting to bear well. What a waste, Charlie, what a stinking waste."

"No, I don't think so, Shara. It sounds glib to say that 'nothing is wasted,' but—well, it's like that dance you just did. Maybe you can't beat gravity—but it surely is a beautiful thing to *try*."

"Yeah, I know. Remember the Light Brigade. Remember the Alamo. They tried." She laughed, a bitter laugh.

"Yes, and so did Jesus of Nazareth. Did you do it for material reward, or because it needed doing? If nothing else, we now have several hundred thousand feet of the most magnificent dance recordings on tape, commercial value zero, real value incalculable, and by me that is no waste. It's over now, and we'll both go do the next thing, but it was *not a waste*." I discovered that I was shouting, and stopped.

She closed her mouth. After a while she tried a smile. "You're right, Charlie. It wasn't a waste. I'm a better dancer than I ever was."

"Damn right. You've transcended choreography."

She smiled ruefully. "Yeah. Even Norrey thinks it's a dead end."

"It is *not* a dead end. There's more to poetry than haiku and sonnets. Dancers don't *have* to be robots, delivering memorized lines with their bodies."

"They do if they want to make a living."

"We'll try again in a few years. Maybe they'll be ready then."

"Sure. Let me get us some drinks."

I slept with her that night, for the first and last time. In the morning I broke down the set in the living room while she packed. I promised to write. I promised to come and visit when I could. I carried her bags down to the car and stowed them inside. I kissed her and waved goodbye. I went looking for a drink, and at four o'clock the next morning a mugger decided I looked drunk enough, and I broke his jaw, his nose, and two ribs and then sat down on him and cried. On Monday morning I showed up at the studio with my hat in my hand and a mouth like a bus-station ashtray and crawled back into my old job. Norrey didn't ask any questions. What with rising food prices, I gave up eating anything but bourbon, and in six months I was fired. It went like that for a long time.

I never did write to her. I kept getting bogged down after "Dear Shara ...."

When I got to the point of selling my video equipment for booze, a relay clicked somewhere and I took stock of myself. The stuff was all the life I had left, and so I went to the local AA instead of the pawnshop and got sober. After a while my soul got numb, and I stopped flinching when I woke up. A hundred times I began to wipe the tapes I still had of Shara—she had copies of her own—but in the end I could not. From time to time I wondered how *she* was doing, and I could not bear to find out. If Norrey heard anything, she didn't tell me about it. She even tried to get me my job back a third time, but it was hopeless. Reputation can be a terrible thing once you've blown it. I was lucky to land a job with an educational TV station in New Brunswick.

It was a long couple of years.

Vidphones were coming out by 1990 and I had breadboarded one of my own without the knowledge or consent of the phone company, which I still hated more than anything. When the peanut bulb that I had replaced the damned bell with started glowing softly on and off one evening in June, I put the receiver on the audio pickup and energized the tube, in case the caller was also equipped. "Hello?"

She was. When Shara's face appeared, I got a cold cube of fear in the pit of my stomach, because I had quit seeing her face everywhere when I quit drinking, and I had been thinking lately of hitting the sauce again. When I blinked and she was still there, I felt a little better and tried to speak. It didn't work.

"Hello, Charlie. It's been a long time."

The second time it worked. "Seems like yesterday. Somebody else's yesterday."

"Yes, it does. It took me *days* to find you. Norrey's in Paris, and no one else knew where you'd gone."

"Yeah. How's farming?"

"I . . . I've put that away, Charlie. It's even more creative than dancing, but it's not the same."

"Then what *are* you doing?"

"Working."

"Dancing?"

"Yes. Charlie, I need you. I mean, I have a job for you. I need your cameras and your eye."

"Never mind the qualifications. Any kind of need will do. *Where are you?* When's the next plane there? Which cameras do I pack?"

"New York, an hour from now, and none of them. I didn't mean 'your cameras' literally—unless you're using GLX-5000s and a Hamilton Board lately."

I whistled. It hurt my mouth. "Not on my budget. Besides, I'm old-fashioned—I like to hold 'em with my hands."

"For this job you'll use a Hamilton, and it'll be a twenty-input Masterchrome, brand new."

"You grew poppies on that farm? Or just struck diamonds with the roto-tiller?"

"You'll be getting paid by Bryce Carrington."

I blinked.

"Now will you catch that plane so I can tell you about it? The New Age, ask for the Presidential Suite."

"The hell with the plane, I'll walk. Quicker." I hung up.

According to the *Time* magazine in my dentist's waiting room, Bryce Carrington was the genius who had become a multimillionaire by convincing a number of giants of industry to underwrite Skyfac, the great orbiting complex that kicked the bottom out of the crystals market. As I recalled the story, some rare polio-like disease had wasted both his legs and put him in a wheelchair. But the legs had lost strength, not function—in lessened gravity, they worked well enough. So he created Skyfac, establishing mining crews on Luna to supply it with cheap raw materials, and lived in orbit under reduced gravity. His picture made him look like a reasonably successful author (as opposed to writer). Other than that I knew nothing about him. I paid little attention to news and none at all to space news.

The New Age was *the* hotel in New York in those days, built on the ruins of the Sheraton. Ultraefficient security, bulletproof windows, carpets thicker than the outside air, and a lobby of an architectural persuasion that John D. MacDonald once called "Early Dental Plate." It stank of money. I was glad I'd made the effort to locate a necktie, and I wished I'd shined my shoes. An incredible man blocked my way as I came in through the airlock. He moved and was built like the toughest, fastest bouncer I ever saw, and he dressed and acted like God's butler. He said his name was Perry. He asked if he could help me, as though he didn't think so.

"Yes, Perry. Would you mind lifting up one of your feet?"

"Why?"

"I'll bet twenty dollars you've shined your soles."

Half his mouth smiled, and he didn't move an inch. "Who did you wish to see?"

"Shara Drummond."

"Not registered."

"The Presidential Suite."

"Oh." Light dawned. "Mr. Carrington's lady. You should have said so. Wait here, please." While he phoned to verify that I was expected, keeping his eye on me and his hand near his pocket, I swallowed my heart and rearranged my face. It took some time. So that was how it was. All right then. That was how it was.

Perry came back and gave me the little button transmitter that would let me walk the corridors of the New Age without being cut down by automatic laser fire, and explained carefully that it would blow a largish hole in me if I attempted to leave the building without returning it. From his manner I gathered that I had just skipped four grades in social standing. I thanked him, though I'm damned if I know why.

I followed the green fluorescent arrows that appeared on the bulbless ceiling, and came after a long and scenic walk to the Presidential Suite. Shara was waiting at the door, in something like an angel's pajamas. It made all that big body look delicate. "Hello, Charlie."

I was jovial and hearty. "Hi, babe. Swell joint. How've you been keeping yourself?"

"I haven't been."

"Well, how's Carrington been keeping you, then?" Steady, boy.

"Come in, Charlie."

I went in. It looked like where the Queen stayed when she was in town, and I'm sure she enjoyed it. You could have landed an airplane in the living room without waking anyone in the bedroom. It had two pianos. Only one fireplace, barely big enough to barbecue a buffalo—you have to scrimp somewhere, I guess. Roger Kellaway was on the quadio, and for a wild moment I thought he was actually in the suite, playing some unseen third piano. So this was how it was.

"Can I get you something, Charlie?"

"Oh, sure. Hash oil, Tangier Supreme. Dom Perignon for the pipe."

30

Without cracking a smile, she went to the cabinet, which looked like a midget cathedral, and produced precisely what I had ordered. I kept my own features impassive and lit up. The bubbles tickled my throat, and the rush was exquisite. I felt myself relaxing, and when we had passed the narghile's mouthpiece a few times I felt her relax. We looked at each other then—really looked at each other—then at the room around us and then at each other again. Simultaneously we roared with laughter, a laughter that blew all the wealth out of the room and let in richness. Her laugh was the same whooping, braying belly laugh I remembered so well, an unselfconscious and lusty laugh, and it reassured me tremendously. I was so relieved I couldn't stop laughing myself, and that kept her going, and just as we might have stopped she pursed her lips and blew a stuttered arpeggio. There's an old recording called the *Spike Jones Laughing Record*, where the tuba player tries to play "The Flight of the Bumblebee" and falls down laughing, and the whole band breaks up and horse-laughs for a full two minutes, and every time they run out of air the tuba player tries another flutter and roars and they all break up again, and once when Shara was blue I bet her ten dollars that she couldn't listen to that record without at least giggling and I won. When I understood now that she was quoting it, I shuddered and dissolved into great whoops of new laughter, and a minute later we had reached the stage where we literally laughed ourselves out of our chairs and lay on the floor in agonies of mirth, weakly pounding the floor and howling. I take that laugh out of my memory now and then and rerun it—but not often, for such records deteriorate drastically with play.

At last we dopplered back down to panting grins, and I helped her to her feet.

"What a perfectly dreadful place," I said, still chuckling.

She glanced around and shuddered. "Oh God, it *is,*

Charlie. It must be awful to need this much front."

"For a horrid while I thought *you* did."

She sobered and met my eyes. "Charlie, I wish I could resent that. In a way I do need it."

My eyes narrowed. "Just what do you mean?"

"I need Bryce Carrington."

"This time you can trot out the qualifiers. *How* do you need him?"

"I need his money," she cried.

How can you relax and tense up at the same time? "Oh, *damn* it, Shara! Is *that* how you're going to get to dance? Buy your way in? What does a critic go for these days?"

"Charlie, stop it. I need Carrington to get seen. He's going to rent me a hall, that's all."

"If that's all, let's get out of the dump right now. I can bor—get enough cash to rent you any hall in the world, and I'm just as willing to risk my money."

"Can you get me Skyfac?"

"Uh?"

I couldn't for the life of me imagine why she proposed to go to Skyfac to dance. Why not Antarctica?

"Shara, you know even less about space than I do, but you must know that a satellite broadcast doesn't have to be made from a satellite?"

"Idiot. It's the setting I want."

I thought about it. "Moon'd be better, visually. Mountains. Light. Contrast."

"The visual aspect is secondary. I don't want one-sixth gee, Charlie. I want zero gravity."

My mouth hung open.

"And I want you to be my video man."

God, she was a rare one. What I needed then was to sit there with my mouth open and think for several minutes. She let me do just that, waiting patiently for me to work it all out.

"Weight isn't a verb anymore, Charlie," she said finally. "That dance ended on the assertion that you can't beat gravity—you said so yourself. Well, that statement is incorrect—obsolete. The dance of the twenty-first century will have to acknowledge that."

"And it's just what you need to make it. A new kind of dance for a new kind of dancer. Unique. It'll catch the public eye, and you should have the field entirely to yourself for years. I like it, Shara. I like it. But can you pull it off?"

"I thought about what you said: that you can't beat gravity but it's beautiful to try. It stayed in my head for months, and then one day I was visiting a neighbor with a TV and I saw newsreels of the crew working on Skyfac Two. I was up all night thinking, and the next morning came up to the States and got a job in Skyfac One. I've been up there for nearly a year, getting next to Carrington. I can do it, Charlie, I can make it work." There was a ripple in her jaw that I had seen before—when she told me off in Le Maintenant. It was a ripple of determination.

Still I frowned. "With Carrington's backing."

Her eyes left mine. "There's no such thing as a free lunch."

"What does he charge?"

She failed to answer, for long enough to answer me. In that instant I began believing in God again, for the first time in years, just to be able to hate Him.

But I kept my mouth shut. She was old enough to manage her own finances. The price of a dream gets higher every year. Hell, I'd half expected it from the moment she'd called me.

But only half.

"Charlie, don't just sit there with your face all knotted up. Say something. Cuss me out, call me a whore, *something*."

"Nuts. You be your own conscience, I have trouble enough being my own. You want to dance, you've got a patron. So now you've got a video man."

I hadn't intended to say that last sentence at all.

Strangely, it almost seemed to disappoint her at first. But then she relaxed and smiled. "Thank you, Charlie. Can you get out of whatever you're doing right away?"

"I'm working for an educational station in Shediac. I even got to shoot some dance footage. A dancing bear from the London Zoo. The amazing thing was how well he danced." She grinned. "I can get free."

"I'm glad. I don't think I could pull this off without you."

"I'm working for you. Not for Carrington."

"All right."

"Where is the great man, anyway? Scuba diving in the bathtub?"

"No," came a quiet voice from the doorway. "I've been skydiving in the lobby."

His wheelchair was a mobile throne. He wore a four-hundred-dollar suit the color of strawberry ice cream, a powder blue turtleneck, and one gold earring. The shoes were genuine leather. The watch was that newfangled bandless kind that literally tells you the time. He wasn't tall enough for her, and his shoulders were absurdly broad, although the suit tried hard to deny both. His eyes were like twin blueberries. His smile was that of a shark wondering which part will taste best. I wanted to crush his head between two boulders.

Shara was on her feet. "Bryce, this is Charles Armstead. I told you—"

"Oh yes. The video chap." He rolled forward and extended an impeccably manicured hand. "I'm Bryce Car-

34

rington, Armstead."

I remained seated, hands in my lap. "Oh yes. The rich chap."

One eyebrow rose an urbane quarter-inch. "Oh my. Another rude one. Well, if you're as good as Shara says you are, you're entitled."

"I'm rotten."

The smile faded. "Let's stop fencing, Armstead. I don't expect manners from creative people, but I have far more significant contempt than yours available if I need any. Now I'm tired of this damned gravity and I've had a rotten day testifying for a friend and it looks like they're going to recall me tomorrow. Do you want the job or don't you?"

He had me there. I did. "Yeah."

"All right, then. Your room is 2772. We'll be going up to Skyfac in two days. Be here at eight A.M."

"I'll want to talk with you about what you'll be needing, Charlie," Shara said. "Give me a call tomorrow."

I whirled to face her, and she flinched from my eyes.

Carrington failed to notice. "Yes, make a list of your requirements by tomorrow, so it can go up with us. Don't scrimp—if you don't fetch it, you'll do without. Good night, Armstead."

I faced him. "Good night, Mr. Carrington." Suh.

He turned toward the narghile, and Shara hurried to refill the chamber and bowl. I turned away hastily and made for the door. My leg hurt so much I nearly fell on the way, but I set my jaw and made it. When I reached the door I said to myself, You will now open the door and go through it, and then I spun on my heel. "Carrington!"

He blinked, surprised to discover I still existed. "Yes?"

"Are you *aware* that she doesn't love you in the slightest? Does that matter to you in any way?" My voice was high, and my fists were surely clenched.

"Oh," he said, and then again, "Oh. So that's what it is. I didn't *think* success alone merited that much contempt." He put down the mouthpiece and folded his fingers together. "Let me tell you something, Armstead. No one has ever loved me, to my knowledge. This suite does not love me." His voice took on human feeling for the first time. "But it is *mine*. Now get out."

I opened my mouth to tell him where to put his job, and then I saw Shara's face, and the pain in it suddenly made me deeply ashamed. I left at once, and when the door closed behind me I vomited on a rug that was worth slightly less than a Hamilton Masterchrome board. I was sorry then that I'd worn a necktie.

The trip to Pike's Peak Spaceport, at least, was aesthetically pleasurable. I enjoy air travel, gliding among stately clouds, watching the rolling procession of mountains and plains, vast jigsaws of farmland, and intricate mosaics of suburbia unfolding below.

But the jump to Skyfac in Carrington's personal shuttle, *That First Step*, might as well have been an old Space Commando rerun. I *know* they can't put portholes in spaceships—but damn it, a shipboard video relay conveys no better resolution, color values, or presence than you get on your living room tube. The only differences are that the stars don't "move" to give the illusion of travel, and there's no director editing the POV to give you dramatically interesting shots.

Aesthetically speaking. The *experiential* difference is that they do not, while you are watching the Space Commando sell hemorrhoid remedies, strap you into a couch, batter you with thunders, make you weigh better than half a ton for an unreasonably long time, and then drop you off the edge of the world into weightlessness. I had been half expecting nausea, but what I got was even more shocking: the sudden, unprecedented, total absence of pain in my leg. At that, Shara was hit worse than I was, barely managing to deploy her dropsickness bag in time. Carrington unstrapped and administered an anti-nausea injection with sure movements. It seemed to take forever to hit her, but when it did there was an enormous change—color and strength returned rapidly, and she was apparently fully recovered by the time the pilot announced that we were commencing docking and would everyone please strap in and shut up. I half expected Carrington to bark manners into him, but apparently the industrial magnate was not that sort of fool. He shut up and strapped himself down.

My leg didn't hurt in the slightest. Not at all.

The Skyfac complex looked like a disorderly heap of bicycle tires and beach balls of various sizes. The one our pilot made for was more like a tractor tire. We matched course, became its axle, and matched spin, and the damned thing grew a spoke that caught us square in the airlock. The airlock was "overhead" of our couches but we entered and left it feet first. A few yards into the spoke, the direction we traveled became "down," and handholds became a ladder. Weight increased with every step, but even when we had emerged in a rather large cubical compartment it was far less than Earth-normal. Nonetheless, my leg resumed biting me.

The room tried to be a classic reception room, high level ("Please be seated. His Majesty will see you shortly."), but the low gee and the p-suits racked along two walls spoiled the effect. Unlike the Space Commando's armor, a real pressure suit looks like nothing so much as a people-shaped baggie, and they look particularly silly in repose. A young dark-haired man in tweed rose from behind a splendidly gadgeted desk and smiled. "Good to see you, Mr. Carrington, I hope you had a pleasant jump."

"Fine thanks, Tom. You remember Shara, of course. This is Charles Armstead. Tom McGillicuddy." We both displayed our teeth and said we were delighted to meet one another. I could see that beneath the pleasantries McGillicuddy was upset about something.

"Nils and Mr. Longmire are waiting in your office, sir. There's . . . there's been another sighting."

"God *damn* it," Carrington began and cut himself off. I stared at him. The full force of my best sarcasm had failed to anger this man. "All right. Take care of my guests while I go hear what Longmire has to say." He started for the door, moving like a beach ball in slow motion but under his own power. "Oh yes—the *Step* is loaded to the gun'ls with bulky equipment, Tom. Have her brought around to the cargo bays. Store the equipment in Six." He left, looking worried. McGillicuddy activated his desk and gave the necessary orders.

"What's going on, Tom?" Shara asked when he was through.

He looked at me before replying. "Pardon my asking, Mr. Armstead, but—are you a newsman?"

"Charlie. No, I'm not. I am a video man, but I work for Shara."

"Mmmm. Well, you'll hear about it sooner or later. About two weeks ago, an object appeared on radar within the orbit of Neptune, just appeared out of nowhere. There were . . . certain other anomalies. It stayed put for half a day and then vanished again. The Space Command slapped a hush on it, but it's common knowledge on board Skyfac."

"And the thing has been sighted again?" Shara asked.

"Just beyond the orbit of Jupiter."

I was only mildly interested. No doubt there was an explanation for the phenomenon, and since Isaac Asimov wasn't around I would doubtless never understand a word of it. Most of us gave up on intelligent nonhuman life when the last intersystem probe came back empty. "Little green men, I suppose. Can you show us the Lounge, Tom? I understand it's just like the one we'll be working in."

He seemed to welcome the change of subject. "Sure thing."

McGillicuddy led us through a p-door opposite the one Carrington had used, through long halls whose floors curved up ahead of and behind us. Each was outfitted differently, each was full of busy, purposeful people, and each reminded me somehow of the lobby of the New Age, or perhaps of the old movie *2001*. Futuristic Opulence, so understated as to fairly shriek. Wall Street lifted bodily into orbit—the *clocks* were on Wall Street time. I tried to make myself believe that cold, empty space lay a short distance away in any direction, but it was impossible. I decided it was a good thing spacecraft didn't have portholes—once he got used to the low gravity, a man might forget and open one to throw out a cigar.

I studied McGillicuddy as we walked. He was immaculate in every respect, from necktie down to nail polish, and he wore no jewelry at all. His hair was short and black, his beard inhibited, and his eyes surprisingly warm in a professionally sterile face. I wondered what he had sold his soul for. I hoped he had gotten his price.

We had to descend two levels to get to the Lounge. The gravity on the upper level was kept at one-sixth normal, partly for the convenience of the Lunar personnel who were Skyfac's only regular commuters, and mostly (of course) for the convenience of Carrington. But descending brought a subtle increase in weight, to nearly a quarter normal. My leg complained bitterly, but I found to my surprise that I preferred the pain to its absence. It's a little scary when an old friend goes away like that.

The Lounge was a larger room than I had expected, quite big enough for our purposes. It encompassed all three levels, and one whole wall was an immense video screen across which stars wheeled dizzily, joined with occasional regularity by a slice of mother Terra. The floor was crowded with chairs and tables in various groupings, but I could see that, stripped, it would provide Shara with entirely adequate room to dance; equally important, my feet told me that it would make a splendid dancing surface. Then I remembered how little use the floor was liable to get.

"Well," Shara said to me with a smile, "this is what home will look like for the next six months. The Ring Two Lounge is identical to this one."

"Six?" McGillicuddy said. "Not a chance."

"What do you mean?" Shara and I said together.

He blinked at our combined volume. "Well, *you* might be good for that long, Charlie. But Shara's already had over a year of low gee, while she was in the typing pool."

"So what?"

"Look, you expect to be in free fall for long periods of time, if I understand this correctly?"

"Twelve hours a day," Shara agreed.

He grimaced. "Shara, I hate to say this . . . but I'll be surprised if you last a month. A body designed for a one-gee environment doesn't work properly in zero gee."

"But it will adapt, won't it?"

He laughed mirthlessly. "Sure. That's why we rotate all personnel Earthside every fourteen months. Your body will adapt. One way. No return. Once you've fully adapted, returning to Earth will stop your heart—if some other major systemic failure doesn't occur first. Look, you were just Earthside for three days—did you have any chest pains? Dizziness? Bowel trouble? Dropsickness on the way up?"

"All of the above," she admitted.

"There you go. You were close to the nominal fourteen-month limit when you left. And your body will adapt even faster under no gravity at all. The free-fall endurance record is ninety days, by the first Skylab crew—and *they* hadn't spent a year in one-sixth gee first, *and* they weren't straining their hearts the way you will be. Hell, there are four men on Luna now, from the original dozen in the first mining team, who will never see Earth again. Eight of their teammates tried. Don't you two know *any*thing about space?"

"But I've got to have at least four months. Four months of solid work, every day. I *must*." She was dismayed but fighting hard for control.

McGillicuddy started to shake his head and then thought better of it. His warm eyes were studying Shara's face. I knew exactly what he was thinking, and I liked him for it.

He was thinking, *How to tell a lovely lady her dearest dream is hopeless?*

He didn't know the half of it. I *knew* how much Shara had already—irrevocably—invested in this dream, and something in me screamed.

And then I saw her jaw ripple and I dared to hope.

Dr. Panzarella was a wiry old man with eyebrows—like two fuzzy caterpillars. He wore a tight-fitting jumpsuit which would not foul a p-suit's seals should he have to get into one in a hurry. His shoulder-length hair, which should have been a mane on the great skull, was tied tightly back against a sudden absence of gravity. A cautious man. To employ an obsolete metaphor, he was a suspenders-*and*-belt type. He looked Shara over, ran tests, and gave her just under a month and a half. Shara said some things. I said some things. McGillicuddy said some things. Panzarella shrugged, made further very careful tests, and reluctantly cut loose of the suspenders. Two months. Not a day over. Possibly less, depending on subsequent monitoring of her body's reactions to extended weightlessness. Then a year Earthside before risking it again. Shara seemed satisfied.

I didn't see how we could do it.

McGillicuddy had assured us that it would take Shara at least a month simply to learn to handle herself competently in zero gee, much less dance. Her familiarity with one-sixth gee would, he predicted, be a liability rather than an asset. Then figure three weeks of choreography and rehearsal, a week of taping and just maybe we could broadcast one dance before Shara had to return to Earth. Not good enough. She and I had calculated that we would need three successive shows, each well received, to make a big enough dent in the dance world for Shara to squeeze into it. A year was far too big a spacing—and *who knew how soon Carrington would tire of her?* So I hollered at Panzarella.

"Mr. Armstead," he said hotly, "I am specifically contractually forbidden to allow this young lady to commit suicide." He grimaced sourly. "I'm told it's terrible public relations."

"Charlie, it's okay," Shara insisted. "I can fit in three dances. We may lose some sleep, but we can do it."

"I once told a man nothing was impossible. He asked me if I could ski through a revolving door. You haven't got . . ."

My brain slammed into hyperdrive, thought about things, kicked itself in the ass a few times, and returned to realtime in time to hear my mouth finish without a break: ". . . much choice, though. Okay, Tom, have that damned Ring Two Lounge cleaned out. I want it naked and spotless, and have

42

somebody paint over that damned video wall, the same shade as the other three and I mean *the same.* Shara, get out of those clothes and into your leotard. Doctor, we'll be seeing you in twelve hours. Quit gaping and *go,* Tom—we'll be going over there at once. *Where the hell are my cameras?*"

McGillicuddy sputtered.

"Get me a torch crew—I'll want holes cut through the walls, cameras behind them, one-way glass, six locations, a room adjacent to the Lounge for a mixer console the size of a jetliner cockpit, and bolt a coffee machine next to the chair. I'll need another room for editing, complete privacy, and total darkness, size of an efficiency kitchen, another coffee machine."

McGillicuddy finally drowned me out. "Mr. *Armstead,* this is the Main Ring of the Skyfac One complex, the administrative offices of one of the wealthiest corporations in existence. If you think this whole Ring is going to stand on its head for you . . ."

So we brought the problem to Carrington. He told McGillicuddy that henceforth, Ring Two was *ours,* as well as any assistance whatsoever that we requested. He looked rather distracted. McGillicuddy started to tell him by how many weeks all this would put off the opening of the Skyfac Two complex. Carrington replied very quietly that he could add and subtract quite well, thank you, and McGillicuddy got white and quiet.

I'll give Carrington that much. He gave us a free hand.

Panzarella ferried over to Skyfac Two with us. We were chauffeured by lean-jawed astronaut types on vehicles looking, for all the world, like pregnant broomsticks. It was as well that we had the doctor with us—Shara fainted on the way over. I nearly did myself, and I'm sure that broomstick has my thigh prints on it yet—falling through space is a scary experience the first time. Shara responded splendidly once we had her inboard again, and fortunately her dropsickness did not return—nausea can be a nuisance in free fall, a disaster in a p-suit. By the time my cameras and mixer had arrived, she was on her feet and sheepish. And while I browbeat a sweating crew of borrowed techs into installing them faster than was humanly possible, Shara began learning how to move in zero gee.

We were ready for the first taping in three weeks.

Living quarters and minimal life support were rigged for us in Ring Two so that we could work around the clock if we chose, but we spent nearly half of our nominal "off hours" in Skyfac One. Shara was required to spend half of three days a week there with Carrington, and spent a sizable portion of her remaining putative sack time out in space, in a p-suit. At first it was a conscious attempt to overcome her gut-level fear of all that emptiness. Soon it became her meditation, her retreat, her artistic reverie—an attempt to gain from contemplation of the cold black depths enough insight into the meaning of extraterrestrial existence to dance of it.

I spent my own time arguing with engineers and electricians and technicians and a damn fool union legate who insisted that the Second Lounge, finished or not, belonged to the hypothetical future crew and administrative personnel. Securing his permission to work there wore the lining off my throat and the insulation off my nerves. Far too many nights I spent slugging instead of sleeping. Minor example: every interior wall in the whole damned Second Ring was painted the identical shade of turquoise—and they couldn't duplicate it to cover that godforsaken video wall in the Lounge. It was McGillicuddy who saved me from gibbering apoplexy—at his suggestion I washed off the third latex job, unshipped the outboard camera that fed the wall screen, brought it inboard, and fixed it to scan an interior wall in an adjoining room. That made us friends again.

It was all like that: jury-rig, improvise, file to fit, and paint to cover. If a camera broke down, I spent sleep time talking with off-shift engineers, finding out what parts in stock could be adapted. It was simply too expensive to have anything shipped up from Earth's immense gravity well, and Luna didn't have what I needed.

At that, Shara worked harder than I did. A body must totally recoordinate itself to function in the absence of weight—she had to forget literally everything she had ever known or learned about dancing and acquire a whole new set of skills. This turned out to be even harder than we had expected. McGillicuddy had been right: what Shara had learned in her year of one-sixth gee was an exaggerated attempt to *retain* terrestrial patterns of coordination— rejecting them altogether was actually easier for *me*.

But I couldn't keep up with her—I had to abandon any thought of handheld camera work and base my plans solely on the six fixed cameras. Fortunately GLX-5000s have a ball-and-socket mount: even behind that damned one-way glass I had about forty degrees of traverse on each one. Learning to coordinate all six simultaneously on the Hamilton Board did a truly extraordinary thing to me—it lifted me that one last step to unity with my art. I found that I could learn to be aware of all six monitors with my mind's eye, to perceive almost spherically, to—not share my attention among the six—to *encompass* them all, seeing like a six-eyed creature from many angles at once. My mind's eye became holographic, my awareness multilayered. I began to really understand, for the first time, three-dimensionality.

It was that fourth dimension that was the kicker. It took Shara two days to decide that she could not possibly become

45

proficient enough in free-fall maneuvering to sustain a half-hour piece in the time required. So she rethought her work plan too, adapting her choreography to the demands of exigency. She put in six hard days under normal Earth weight.

And for her, too, the effort brought her that one last step toward apotheosis.

On Monday of the fourth week we began taping *Liberation.*

Establishing shot:

A great turquoise box, seen from within. Dimensions unknown, but the color somehow lends an impression of immensity, of vast distances. Against the far wall, a swinging pendulum attests that this is a standard-gravity environment; but the pendulum swings so slowly and is so featureless in construction that it is impossible to estimate its size and so extrapolate that of the room.

Because of this trompe l'oeil effect, the room seems rather smaller than it really is when the camera pulls back and we are wrenched into proper perspective by the appearance of Shara, prone, inert, face down on the floor, facing us.

She wears beige leotard and tights. Hair the color of fine mahogany is pulled back into a loose ponytail which fans across one shoulder blade. She does not appear to breathe. She does not appear to be alive.

Music begins. The aging Mahavishnu, on obsolete nylon acoustic, establishes a minor E in no hurry at all. A pair of small candles in simple brass holders appear, inset on either side of the room. They are larger than life, though small beside Shara. Both are unlit.

Her body . . . there is no word. It does not move, in the sense of motor activity. One might say that a ripple passes through it, save that the motion is clearly all outward from

46

her center. She *swells,* as if the first breath of life was being taken by her whole body at once. She lives.

The twin wicks begin to glow, oh, softly. The music takes on quiet urgency.

Shara raises her head to us. Her eyes focus somewhere beyond the camera yet short of infinity. Her body writhes, undulates, and the glowing wicks are coals (that this brightening takes place in slow motion is not apparent).

A violent contraction raises her to a crouch, spilling the ponytail across her shoulder. Mahavishnu begins a cyclical cascade of runs, in increasing tempo. Long, questing tongues of yellow-orange flame begin to blossom *downward* from the twin wicks, whose coals are turning to blue.

The contraction's release flings her to her feet. The twin skirts of flame about the wicks curl up over themselves, writhing furiously, to become conventional candle flames, flickering now in normal time. Tablas, tambouras, and a bowed string bass join the guitar, and they segue into an energetic interplay around a minor seventh that keeps trying, fruitlessly, to find resolution in the sixth. The candles stay in perspective but dwindle in size until they vanish.

Shara begins to explore the possibilities of motion. First she moves only perpendicular to the camera's line of sight, exploring that dimension. Every motion of arms or legs or head is clearly seen to be a defiance of gravity, of a force as inexorable as radioactive decay, as entropy itself. The most violent surges of energy succeed only for a time—the outflung leg falls, the outthrust arm drops. She must struggle or fall. She pauses in thought.

Her hands and arms reach out toward the camera, and at the instant they do we cut to a view from the left-hand wall. Seen from the right side, she reaches out into this new dimension and soon begins to move in it. (As she moves backward out of the camera's field, its entire image shifts right on our screen, butted out of the way by the incoming image of a second camera, which picks her up as the first loses her without a visible seam.)

The new dimension too fails to fulfill Shara's desire for freedom from gravity. Combining the two, however, presents so many permutations of movement that for a while, intoxicated, she flings herself into experimentation. In the next fifteen minutes, Shara's entire background and history in dance are recapitulated in a blinding tour de force that incorporates elements of jazz, modern, and the more graceful aspects of Olympic-level mat gymnastics. Five cameras come into play, singly and in pairs on split-screen, as the "bag of tricks" amassed in a lifetime of study and improvisation are rediscovered and performed by a superbly trained and versatile body, in a pyrotechnic display that would shout of joy if her expression did not remain aloof, almost arrogant. *This is the offering,* she seems to say, *which you would not accept. This, by itself, was not good enough.*

And it is not. Even in its raging energy and total control, her body returns again and again to the final compromise of mere erectness, that last simple refusal to fall.

Clamping her jaw, she works into a series of leaps, ever longer, ever higher. She seems at last to hang suspended for full seconds, straining to fly. When, inevitably, she falls, she falls reluctantly, only at the last possible instant tucking and rolling back onto her feet. The musicians are in a crescendoing frenzy. We see her now only with the single original camera, and the twin candles have returned, small but burning fiercely.

The leaps begin to diminish in intensity and height, and she takes longer to build to each one. She has been dancing flat out for nearly twenty minutes: as the candle flames begin to wane, so does her strength. At last she retreats to a place beneath the indifferent pendulum, gathers herself with a final desperation, and races forward toward us. She reaches incredible speed in a short space, hurls herself into a double roll, and bounds up into the air off one foot, seeming a full second later to push off against empty air for a few more inches of height. Her body goes rigid, her eyes and mouth gape wide, the flames reach maximum brilliance, the music peaks with the tortured wail of an electric guitar, and—she falls, barely snapping into a roll in time, rising only as far as a crouch. She holds there for a long moment, and gradually her head and shoulders slump, defeated, toward the floor. The candle flames draw in upon themselves in a curious way and appear to go out. The string bass saws on, modulating down to D.

Muscle by muscle, Shara's body gives up the struggle. The air seems to tremble around the wicks of the candles, which have now grown nearly as tall as her crouching form.

Shara lifts her face to the camera with evident effort. Her face is anguished, her eyes nearly shut. A long beat.

All at once she opens her eyes wide, squares her shoulders, and contracts. It is the most exquisite and total contraction ever dreamed of, filmed in realtime but seeming almost to be in slow motion. She holds it. Mahavishnu comes back in on guitar, building in increasing tempo from a downtuned bass string to a D with a flatted fourth. Shara holds.

We shift for the first time to an overhead camera, looking down on her from a great height. As Mahavishnu's picking increases to the point where the chord seems a sustained drone, Shara slowly lifts her head, still holding the contraction, until she is staring directly up at us. She poises there for an eternity, like a spring wound to the bursting point . . .

. . . and explodes upward toward us, rising higher and

faster than she possibly can in a soaring flight that *is* slow motion now, coming closer and closer until her hands disappear off either side and her face fills the screen, flanked by two candles which have bloomed into gouts of yellow flame in an instant. The guitar and bass are submerged in an orchestra.

Almost at once she whirls away from us, and the POV switches to the original camera, on which we see her fling herself down ten meters to the floor, reversing her attitude in midflight and twisting. She comes out of her roll in an absolutely flat trajectory that takes her the length of the room. She hits the far wall with a crash audible even over the music, shattering the still pendulum. Her thighs soak up the kinetic energy and then release it, and once again she is racing toward us, hair streaming straight out behind her, a broad smile of triumph growing larger in the screen.

In the next five minutes all six cameras vainly try to track her as she caroms around the immense room like a hummingbird trying to batter its way out of a cage, using the walls, floor, and ceiling the way a jai alai master does, *existing in three dimensions.* Gravity is defeated. The basic assumption of all dance is transcended.

Shara is transformed.

She comes to rest at last at vertical center in the forefront of the turquoise cube, arms-legs-fingers-toes-face straining *outward,* turning gently end over end. All four cameras that bear on her join in a four-way split-screen, the orchestra resolves into its final E major, and—fadeout.

I had neither the time nor the equipment to create the special effects that Shara wanted. So I figured out ways to warp reality to my need. The first candle segment was a twinned shot of a candle being blown out from above—in ultraslow motion, and in reverse. The second segment was a simple recording of reality. I had lit the candle, started taping—and had the Ring's spin killed. A candle behaves oddly in zero gee. The low-density combustion gases do not rise up from the flame, allowing air to reach it from beneath. The flame does not go out: it becomes dormant. Restore gravity within a minute or so, and it blooms back to life again. All I did was monkey with speeds a bit to match in with the music and Shara's dance. I got the idea from the foreman of the metal shop where we were designing things Shara would need for the next dance.

I set up a screen in the Ring One Lounge, and everyone in Skyfac who could cut work crowded in for the broadcast. They saw exactly what was being sent out over worldwide satellite hookup (Carrington had sufficient pull to arrange twenty-five minutes without commercial interruption) almost a full half-second before the world did.

I spent the broadcast in the Communications Room chewing my fingernails. But it went without a hitch, and I slapped my board dead and made it to the Lounge in time to see the last half of the standing ovation. Shara stood before the screen, Carrington sitting beside her, and I found the difference in their expressions instructive. Her face showed no surprise or modesty. She had had faith in herself throughout, had approved this tape for broadcast—she was aware, with that incredible detachment of which so few artists are capable, that the wild applause was only what she deserved. But her face showed that she was deeply surprised—and deeply grateful—to be given what she deserved.

Carrington, on the other hand, registered a triumph strangely mingled with relief. He too had faith in Shara, backing it with a large investment—but his faith was that of a businessman in a gamble he believes will pay off, and as I watched his eyes and the glisten of sweat on his forehead, I realized that no businessman ever takes an expensive gamble without worrying that it may be the fiasco that will begin the loss of his only essential commodity: face.

Seeing his kind of triumph next to hers spoiled the moment for me, and instead of thrilling for Shara I found myself almost hating her. She spotted me and waved me to join her before the cheering crowd, but I turned and literally flung myself from the room. I borrowed a bottle from the metal-shop foreman and got stinking.

The next morning my head felt like a fifteen-amp fuse on a forty-amp circuit, and I seemed to be held together only by surface tension.

Sudden movements frightened me. It's a long fall off that wagon, even at one-sixth gee.

The phone chimed—I hadn't had time to rewire it—and a young man I didn't know politely announced that Mr. Carrington wished to see me in his office. At once. I spoke of a barbed-wire suppository, and what Mr. Carrington might do with it, at once. Without changing expression, he repeated his message and disconnected.

So I crawled into my clothes, decided to grow a beard, and left. Along the way I wondered what I had traded my independence for, and why?

Carrington's office was oppressively tasteful, but at least the lighting was subdued. Best of all, its filter system would handle smoke—the sweet musk of pot lay on the air. I accepted a macrojoint of "Maoi-Zowie" from Carrington with something approaching gratitude and began melting my hangover.

Shara sat next to his desk, wearing a leotard and a layer of sweat. She had obviously spent the morning rehearsing for the next dance. I felt ashamed, and consequently snappish, avoiding her eyes and her hello. Panzarella and McGillicuddy came in on my heels, chattering about the latest sighting of the mysterious object from deep space, which had appeared this time in the neighborhood of Mercury. They were arguing over whether it displayed signs of sentience or not, and I wished they'd shut up.

Carrington waited until we had all seated ourselves and lit up, then rested a hip on his desk and smiled. "Well, Tom?"

McGillicuddy beamed. "Better than we expected, sir. All the ratings agree we had about 74 percent of the world audience."

"The hell with the Nielsens," I snapped. *What did the critics say?*"

McGillicuddy blinked. "Well, the general reaction so far is that Shara was a smash. The *Times*—"

I cut him off again. "What was the less than general reaction?"

"Well, nothing is ever unanimous."

"Specifics. The dance press? Liz Zimmer? Migdalski?"

"Uh. Not as good. Praise, yes—only a blind man could've panned that show. But guarded praise. Uh, Zimmer called it a magnificent dance spoiled by a gimmicky ending."

"And Migdalski?" I insisted.

"He headed his review 'But What Do You Do for an Encore?' " McGillicuddy admitted. "His basic thesis was that it was a charming one-shot. But the *Times*—"

"Thank you, Tom," Carrington said quietly. "About what we expected, isn't it, my dear? A big splash, but no one's willing to call it a tidal wave yet."

She nodded. "But they will, Bryce. The next two dances will sew it up."

Panzarella spoke up. "Ms. Drummond, may I ask why you played it the way you did? Using the null-gee interlude only as a brief adjunct to conventional dance—surely you must have expected the critics to call it gimmickry."

Shara smiled and answered: "To be honest, Doctor, I had no choice. I'm learning to use my body in free fall, but it's still a conscious effort, almost a pantomime. I need another few weeks to make it second nature, and it *has* to be if I'm to sustain a whole piece in it. So I dug a conventional dance out of the trunk, tacked on a five-minute ending that used every zero-gee move I knew, and found to my extreme relief that they made thematic sense together. I told Charlie my notion, and he made it work visually and dramatically—that whole business of the candles was his, and it underlined what I was trying to say better than any set we could have built."

"So you have not yet completed what you came here to do?" Panzarella asked Shara.

"Oh, no. Not by any means. The next dance will show the world that dance is more than controlled falling. And the third . . . the third will be what this has all been for." Her face lit, became animated. "The third dance will be the one I have wanted to dance all my life. I can't entirely picture it, yet—but I know that when I become capable of dancing it, I will create it, and it will be my greatest dance."

Panzarella cleared his throat. "How long will it take you?"

"Not long," she said. "I'll be ready to tape the next dance in two weeks, and I can start on the last one almost at once. With luck, I'll have it in the can before my month is up."

"Ms. Drummond," Panzarella said gravely, "I'm afraid you don't have another month."

Shara went white as snow, and I half rose from my seat. Carrington looked intrigued.

"How much time?" Shara asked.

"Your latest tests have not been encouraging. I had assumed that the sustained exercise of rehearsal and practice would tend to slow your system's adaptation. But most of your work has been in total weightlessness, and I failed to realize the extent to which your body is accustomed to sustained exertion—in a terrestrial environment."

"How much time?"

"Two weeks. Possibly three, if you spend three separate hours a day at hard exercise in two gravities."

"That's ridiculous," I burst out. "We can't start and stop the Ring six times a day, and even if we could she could break a leg in two gees."

"I've got to have four weeks," Shara said.

"Ms. Drummond, I am sorry."

"I've got to have four weeks."

Panzarella had that same look of helpless sorrow that McGillicuddy and I had had in our turn, and I was suddenly sick to death of a universe in which people had to keep looking at Shara that way. "Dammit," I roared, "she needs four weeks."

Panzarella shook his shaggy head. "If she stays in zero gee for four working weeks, she may die."

Shara sprang from her chair. "Then I'll die," she cried. "I'll take that chance. I *have* to."

Carrington coughed. "I'm afraid I can't permit you to, darling."

She whirled on him furiously.

"This dance of yours is excellent PR for Skyfac," he said calmly, "but if it were to kill you it might boomerang, don't you think?"

Her mouth worked, and she fought desperately for control. My own head whirled. Die? Shara?

"Besides," he added, "I've grown quite fond of you."

"Then I'll stay up here in low-gee," she burst out.

"Where? The only areas of sustained weightlessness are

factories, and you're not qualified to work in one."

"Then for God's sake give me one of the new pods, the small spheres. Bryce, I'll give you a higher return on your investment than a factory pod, and I'll . . ." Her voice changed. "I'll be available to you always."

He smiled lazily. "Yes, but I might not *want* you always, darling. My mother warned me strongly against making irrevocable decisions about women. Especially informal ones. Besides, I find zero-gee sex rather too exhausting as a steady diet."

I had almost found my voice and now I lost it again. I was glad Carrington was turning her down—but the way he did it made me yearn to drink his blood.

Shara too was speechless for a time. When she spoke, her voice was low, intense, almost pleading. "Bryce, it's a matter of timing. If I broadcast two more dances in the next four weeks, I'll have a world to return to. If I have to go Earthside and wait a year or two, that third dance will sink without a trace—no one'll be looking, and they won't have the memory of the first two. This is my only option, *Bryce—let me take the chance*. Panzarella can't guarantee four weeks will kill me."

"I can't guarantee your survival," the doctor said.

"You can't guarantee that any one of us will live out the day," she snapped. She whirled back to Carrington, held him with her eyes. "Bryce, *let me risk it*." Her face underwent a massive effort, produced a smile that put a knife through my heart. "I'll make it worth your while."

Carrington savored that smile and the utter surrender in her voice like a man enjoying a fine claret. I wanted to slay him with my hands and teeth, and I prayed that he would add the final cruelty of turning her down. But I had underestimated his true capacity for cruelty.

"Go ahead with your rehearsal, my dear," he said at last.

"We'll make a final decision when the time comes. I shall have to think about it."

I don't think I've ever felt so hopeless, so . . . impotent in my life. Knowing it was futile, I said, "Shara, I can't let you risk your life—"

"I'm going to do this, Charlie," she cut me off, "with or without you. No one else knows my work well enough to tape it properly, but if you want out I can't stop you." Carrington watched me with detached interest. "Well?"

I said a filthy word. "You know the answer."

"Then let's get to work."

Tyros are transported on the pregnant broomsticks. Old hands hang outside the airlock, dangling from handholds on the outer surface of the spinning Ring. They face in the direction of the spin, and when their destination comes under the horizon, they just drop off. Thruster units built into gloves and boots supply the necessary course corrections. The distances involved are small. Shara and I, having spent more weightless hours than some technicians who'd been in Skyfac for years, were old hands. We made scant and efficient use of our thrusters, chiefly in canceling the energy imparted to us by the spin of the Ring we left. We had throat mikes and hearing-aid-size receivers, but there was no conversation on the way across the void. I spent the journey appreciating the starry emptiness through which I fell—I had come, perforce, to understand the attraction of sky-diving—and wondering whether I would ever get used to the cessation of pain in my leg. It even seemed to hurt less under spin those days.

We grounded, with much less force than a sky-diver does, on the surface of the new studio. It was an enormous steel globe, studded with sunpower screens and heat-losers, tethered to three more spheres in various stages of construction

on which p-suited figures were even now working. Mc-
Gillicuddy had told me that the complex when completed
would be used for "controlled density processing," and when
I said, "How nice," he added, "Dispersion forming and vari-
able density casting," as if that explained everything. Perhaps
it did. Right at the moment, it was Shara's studio.

The airlock led to a rather small working space around a
smaller interior sphere some fifty meters in diameter. It too
was pressurized, intended to contain a vacuum, but its locks
stood open. We removed our p-suits, and Shara unstrapped
her thruster bracelets from a bracing strut and put them on,
hanging by her ankles from the strut while she did so. The
anklets went on next. As jewelry they were a shade bulky—
but they had twenty minutes' continuous use each, and their
operation was not visible in normal atmosphere and lighting.
Zero-gee dance without them would have been enormously
more difficult.

As she was fastening the last strap I drifted over in front of
her and grabbed the strut. "Shara . . ."

"Charlie, I can beat it. I'll exercise in *three* gravities, and
I'll sleep in two, and I'll make this body last. I know I can."

"You could skip *Mass Is a Verb* and go right to the
Stardance."

She shook her head. "I'm not ready yet—and neither is the
audience. I've got to lead myself and them through dance in a
sphere first—in a contained space—before I'll be ready to
dance in empty space, or for them to appreciate it. I have to
free my mind, and theirs, from just about every preconcep-
tion of dance, change the postulates. Even two stages is too
few—but it's the irreducible minimum." Her eyes softened.
"Charlie—I must."

"I know," I said gruffly and turned away. Tears are a nuisance in free fall—they don't *go* anywhere. I began hauling

myself around the surface of the inner sphere toward the camera emplacement I was working on, and Shara entered the inner sphere to begin rehearsal.

I prayed as I worked on my equipment, snaking cables among the bracing struts and connecting them to drifting terminals. For the first time in years I prayed, prayed that Shara would make it. That we both would.

The next twelve days were the toughest of my life. Shara worked twice as hard as I did. She spent half of every day working in the studio, half of the rest in exercise under two and a quarter gravities (the most Dr. Panzarella would permit), and half of the rest in Carrington's bed, trying to make him contented enough to let her stretch her time limit. Perhaps she slept in the few hours left over. I only know that she never looked tired, never lost her composure or her dogged determination. Stubbornly, reluctantly, her body lost its awkwardness, took on grace even in an environment where grace required enormous concentration. Like a child learning to walk, Shara learned how to fly.

I even began to get used to the absence of pain in my leg.

What can I tell you of *Mass* if you have not seen it? It cannot be described, even badly, in mechanistic terms, the way a symphony could be written out in words. Conventional dance terminology is, by its built-in assumptions, worse than useless, and if you are at all familiar with the new nomenclature you *must* be familiar with *Mass Is a Verb*, from which it draws *its* built-in assumptions.

Nor is there much I can say about the technical aspects of *Mass*. There were no special effects, not even music. Brindle's superb score was composed *from the dance* and added to the tape with my permission two years later, but it was for the original, silent version that I was given the Emmy. My entire contribution, aside from editing, and installing the two trampolines, was to camouflage batteries of wide-dispersion light sources in clusters around each camera eye and wire them so that they energized only when they were out of frame with respect to whichever camera was on at the time—ensuring that Shara was always lit from the front, presenting two (not always congruent) shadows. I made no attempt to employ flashy camera work; I simply recorded what Shara danced, changing POV only as she did.

No, *Mass Is a Verb* can be described only in symbolic terms, and then poorly. I can say that Shara demonstrated that mass and inertia are as able as gravity to supply the dynamic conflict essential to dance. I can tell you that from them she distilled a kind of dance that could only have been imagined by a group-head consisting of an acrobat, a stunt-diver, a sky-writer, and an underwater ballerina. I can tell you that she dismantled the last interface between herself and utter freedom of motion, subduing her body to her will and space itself to her need.

And still I will have told you next to nothing. For Shara sought more than freedom—she sought meaning. *Mass* was, above all, a spiritual event—its title pun paralleling its thematic ambiguity between the technological and the theological. Shara made the human confrontation with existence a transitive act, literally meeting God halfway. I do not mean to imply that her dance at any time addressed an exterior God, a discrete entity with or without white beard. Her dance addressed reality, gave successive expression to the Three Eternal Questions asked by every human being who ever lived.

Her dance observed her *self* and asked, *"How have I come to be here?"*

Her dance observed the universe in which self existed, and

asked, *"How did all this come to be here with me?"*

And at last, observing her self in relation to its universe, *"Why am I so alone?"*

And having asked these questions, having earnestly asked them with every muscle and sinew she possessed, she paused, hung suspended in the center of the sphere, her body and soul open to the universe, and when no answer came, she contracted. Not in a dramatic ceiling-spring sense, as she had in *Liberation*, a compressing of energy and tension. This was physically similar, but an utterly different phenomenon. It was a focusing inward, an act of introspection, a turning of the mind's (soul's?) eye in upon itself, to seek answers that lay nowhere else. Her body too, therefore, seemed to fold in upon itself, compacting her mass so evenly that her position in space was not disturbed.

And reaching within herself, she closed on emptiness. The camera faded out, leaving her alone, rigid, encapsulated, yearning. The dance ended, leaving her three questions unanswered, the tension of their asking unresolved. Only the expression of patient waiting on her face blunted the shocking edge of the non-ending, made it bearable, a small blessed sign whispering, "To be continued."

By the eighteenth day we had it in the can in rough form. Shara put it immediately out of her mind and began choreographing *Stardance*, but I spent two hard days of editing before I was ready to release the tape for broadcast. I had four days until the half-hour of prime time Carrington had purchased—but that wasn't the deadline I felt breathing down the back of my neck.

McGillicuddy came into my workroom while I was editing, and although he saw the tears running down my face he said no word. I let the tape run, and he watched in silence, and soon his face was wet, too. When the tape had been over for a long time he said, very softly, "One of these days I'm going to have to quit this stinking job."

I said nothing.

"I used to be a karate instructor. I was pretty good. I could teach again, maybe do exhibition work, make ten percent of what I do now."

I said nothing.

"The whole damned Ring's bugged, Charlie. The desk in my office can activate and tap any vidphone in Skyfac. Four at a time, actually."

I said nothing.

"I saw you both in the airlock, when you came back the last time. I saw her collapse. I saw you bringing her around. I heard her make you promise not to tell Dr. Panzarella."

I waited. Hope stirred.

He dried his face. "I came in here to tell you I was going to Panzarella, to tell him what I saw. He'd bully Carrington into sending her home right away."

"And now?" I said.

"I've seen that tape."

"And you know the *Stardance* will probably kill her?"

"Yes."

"And you know we have to let her do it?"

"Yes."

Hope died. I nodded. "Then get out of here and let me work."

He left.

On Wall Street and aboard Skyfac it was late afternoon when I finally had the tape edited to my satisfaction. I called Carrington, told him to expect me in half an hour, showered, shaved, dressed, and left.

A major of the Space Command was there with him when

I arrived, but he was not introduced and so I ignored him. Shara was there too, wearing a thing made of orange smoke that left her breasts bare. Carrington had obviously made her wear it, as an urchin writes filthy words on an altar, but she wore it with a perverse and curious dignity that I sensed annoyed him. I looked her in the eye and smiled. "Hi, kid. It's a good tape."

"Let's see," Carrington said. He and the major took seats behind the desk, and Shara sat beside it.

I fed the tape into the video rig built into the office wall, dimmed the lights, and sat across from Shara. It ran twenty minutes, uninterrupted, no soundtrack, stark naked.

It was terrific.

Aghast is a funny word. To make you aghast, a thing must hit you in a place you haven't armored over with cynicism yet. I seem to have been born cynical; I have been aghast three times that I can remember. The first was when I learned, at the age of three, that there were people who could deliberately hurt kittens. The second was when I learned, at age seventeen, that there were people who could actually take LSD and then hurt other people for fun. The third was when *Mass Is a Verb* ended and Carrington said in perfectly conversational tones, "Very pleasant, very graceful. I like it"; then I learned, at age forty-five, that there were men, not fools or cretins but intelligent men, who could watch Shara Drummond dance and fail to *see*. We all, even the most cynical of us, always have some illusion which we cherish.

Shara simply let it bounce off her somehow, but I could see that the major was as aghast as I, controlling his features with a visible effort.

Suddenly welcoming a distraction from my horror and dismay, I studied him more closely, wondering for the first time what he was doing here. He was my age, lean and more hard-bitten than I am, with silver fuzz on top of his skull and an extremely tidy mustache on the front. I'd taken him for a crony of Carrington's, but three things changed my mind. Something indefinable about his eyes told me that he was a military man of long combat experience. Something equally indefinable about his carriage told me that he was on duty at the moment. And something quite definable about the line his mouth made told me that he was disgusted with the duty he had drawn.

When Carrington went on, "What do you think, Major?" in polite tones, the man paused for a moment, gathering his thoughts and choosing his words. When he did speak, it was not to Carrington.

"Ms. Drummond," he said quietly, "I am Major William Cox, commander of S.C. *Champion*, and I am honored to meet you. That was the most profoundly moving thing I have ever seen."

Shara thanked him most gravely. "This is Charles Armstead, Major Cox. He made the tape."

Cox regarded me with new respect. "A magnificent job, Mr. Armstead." He stuck out his hand and I shook it.

Carrington was beginning to understand that we three shared a thing which excluded him. "I'm glad you enjoyed it, Major," he said with no visible trace of sincerity. "You can see it again on your television tomorrow night, if you chance to be off duty. And eventually, of course, cassettes will be made available. Now perhaps we can get to the matter at hand."

Cox's face closed as if it had been zipped up, became stiffly formal. "As you wish, sir."

Puzzled, I began what I thought was the matter at hand. "I'd like your own Comm Chief to supervise the actual transmission this time, Mr. Carrington. Shara and

I will be too busy to—"

"My Comm Chief will supervise the broadcast, Armstead," Carrington interrupted, "but I don't think you'll be particularly busy."

I was groggy from lack of sleep; my uptake was rather slow.

He touched his desk delicately. "McGillicuddy, report at once," he said, and released it. "You see, Armstead, you and Shara are both returning to Earth. At once."

"*What?*"

"Bryce, you *can't*," Shara cried. "You *promised*."

"I promised I would think about it, my dear," he corrected.

"The hell you say. That was weeks ago. Last night you *promised*."

"Did I? My dear, there were no witnesses present last night. Altogether for the best, don't you agree?"

I was speechless with rage.

McGillicuddy entered. "Hello, Tom," Carrington said pleasantly. "You're fired. You'll be returning to Earth at once, with Ms. Drummond and Mr. Armstead, aboard Major Cox's vessel. Departure in one hour, and don't leave anything you're fond of." He glanced from McGillicuddy to me. "From Tom's desk you can tap any vidphone in Skyfac. From my desk you can tap Tom's desk."

Shara's voice was low. "Bryce, two days. God damn you, name your price."

He smiled slightly. "I'm sorry, darling. When informed of your collapse, Dr. Panzarella became most specific. Not even one more day. Alive you are a distinct plus for Skyfac's image—you are my gift to the world. Dead you are an albatross around my neck. I cannot allow you to die on my property. I anticipated that you might resist leaving, and so I

spoke to a friend in the"—he glanced at Cox—"*higher* eche-
lons of the Space Command, who was good enough to send
the major here to escort you home. You are not under arrest
in the legal sense—but I assure you that you have no choice.
Something like protective custody applies. Goodbye, Shara."
He reached for a stack of reports on his desk, and I surprised
myself considerably.

I cleared the desk entirely, tucked head catching him
squarely in the sternum. His chair was bolted to the deck and
so it snapped clean. I recovered so well that I had time for one
glorious right. Do you know how, if you punch a basketball
squarely, it will bounce up from the floor? That's what his
head did, in low-gee slow motion.

Then Cox had hauled me to my feet and shoved me into
the far corner of the room. "Don't," he said to me, and his
voice must have held a lot of that "habit of command" they
talk about, because it stopped me cold. I stood breathing in
great gasps while Cox helped Carrington to his feet.

The millionaire felt his smashed nose, examined the blood
on his fingers, and looked at me with raw hatred. "You'll
never work in video again, Armstead. You're through. Finished. Unemployed, you get that?"

Cox tapped him on the shoulder, and Carrington spun on
him. "What the hell do you want?" he barked.

Cox smiled. "Carrington, my late father once said, 'Bill,
make your enemies by choice, not by accident.' Over the
years I have found that to be excellent advice. You suck."

"And not particularly well," Shara agreed.

Carrington blinked. Then his absurdly broad shoulders
swelled and he roared, "Out, all of you! *Off my property at
once!*"

By unspoken consent, we waited for McGillicuddy, who
knew his cue. "Mr. Carrington, it is a rare privilege and a

great honor to have been fired by you. I shall think of it always as a Pyrrhic defeat." And he half bowed and we left, each buoyed by a juvenile feeling of triumph that must have lasted ten seconds.

The sensation of falling that comes with zero gee is literal truth, but your body quickly learns to treat it as an illusion. Now, in zero gee for the last time, for the half hour before I would be back in Earth's own gravitational field, I felt I was falling. Plummeting into some bottomless gravity well, dragged down by the anvil that was my heart, the scraps of a dream that should have held me aloft fluttering overhead.

The *Champion* was three times the size of Carrington's yacht, which childishly pleased me until I recalled that he had summoned it here without paying for either fuel or crew. A guard at the airlock saluted as we entered. Cox led us to a compartment aft of the airlock where we were to strap in. He noticed along the way that I used only my left hand to pull myself along, and when we stopped, he said, "Mr. Armstead, my late father also told me, 'Hit the soft parts with your hand. Hit the hard parts with a utensil.' Otherwise I can find no fault with your technique. I wish I could shake your hand."

I tried to smile, but I didn't have it in me. "I admire your taste in enemies, Major."

"A man can't ask for more. I'm afraid I can't spare time to have your hand looked at until we've grounded. We begin re-entry immediately."

"Forget it."

He bowed to Shara, did *not* tell her how deeply sorry he was to, et cetera, wished us all a comfortable journey, and left. We strapped into our acceleration couches to await ignition. There ensued a long and heavy silence, compounded of a mutual sadness that bravado could only have underlined.

We did not look at each other, as though our combined sorrow might achieve some kind of critical mass. Grief struck us dumb, and I believe that remarkably little of it was self-pity.

But then a whole lot of time seemed to have gone by. Quite a bit of intercom chatter came faintly from the next compartment, but ours was not in circuit. At last we began to talk, desultorily, discussing the probable critical reaction to *Mass Is a Verb*, whether analysis was worthwhile or the theater really dead, anything at all except future plans. Eventually there was nothing else to talk about, so we shut up again. I guess I'd say we were in shock.

For some reason I came out of it first. "What in hell is taking them so long?" I barked irritably.

McGillicuddy started to say something soothing, then glanced at his watch and yelped. "You're right. It's been nearly an hour."

I looked at the wall clock, got hopelessly confused until I realized it was on Greenwich time rather than Wall Street, and realized he was correct. "Chrissakes," I shouted, "the whole bloody *point* of this exercise is to protect Shara from overexposure to free fall! I'm going forward."

"Charlie, hold it." McGillicuddy, with two good hands, unstrapped faster than I. "Dammit, stay right there and cool off. I'll go find out what the holdup is."

He was back in a few minutes, and his face was slack. "We're not going anywhere. Cox has orders to sit tight."

"What? Tom, what the *hell* are you talking about?"

His voice was all funny. "Red fireflies. More like bees, actually. In a balloon."

He simply *could not* be joking with me, which meant he flat out *had* to have gone completely round the bend, which meant that somehow I had blundered into my favorite nightmare where everyone but me goes crazy and begins gibbering at me. So I lowered my head like an enraged bull and charged out of the room so fast the door barely had time to get out of my way.

It just got worse. When I reached the door to the bridge I was going much too fast to be stopped by anything short of a body block, and the crewmen present were caught flatfooted. There was a brief flurry at the door, and then I was on the bridge, and then I decided that I had gone crazy too, which somehow made everything all right.

The forward wall of the bridge was one enormous video tank—and just enough off center to faintly irritate me, standing out against the black deep as clearly as cigarettes in a darkroom, there truly did swarm a multitude of red fireflies.

The conviction of unreality made it okay. But then Cox snapped me back to reality with a bellowed *"Off this bridge, mister."* If I'd been in a normal frame of mind it would have blown me out the door and into the farthest corner of the ship; in my current state it managed to jolt me into acceptance of the impossible situation. I shivered like a wet dog and turned to him.

"Major," I said desperately, "what is going on?"

As a king may be amused by an insolent varlet who refuses to kneel, he was bemused by the phenomenon of someone failing to obey him. It bought me an answer. "We are confronting intelligent alien life," he said concisely. "I believe them to be sentient plasmoids."

I had never for a moment believed that the mysterious object which had been leapfrogging around the solar system since I came to Skyfac was *alive.* I tried to take it in, then abandoned the task and went back to my main priority. "I don't care if they're eight tiny reindeer; you've got to get this can back to Earth *now.*"

"Sir, this vessel is on Emergency Red Alert and on Combat Standby. At this moment the suppers of everyone in North America are getting cold. I will consider myself fortunate if I ever see Earth again. Now get off my bridge."

"But you don't *understand*. Sustained free fall might kill Shara. That's what you came up here to prevent, dammit. . . ."

"MISTER ARMSTEAD! This is a military vessel. We are facing nearly a dozen intelligent beings who appeared out of hyperspace near here twenty minutes ago, beings who therefore use a drive beyond my conception with no visible parts. If it makes you feel any better I am aware that I have a passenger aboard of greater intrinsic value to my species than this ship and everyone else on her, and if it is any comfort to you this knowledge already provides a distraction I need like an auxiliary anus, and I can no more leave this orbit than I can grow horns. Now will you get off this bridge or will you be dragged?"

I didn't get a chance to decide; they dragged me.

On the other hand, by the time I got back to our compartment, Cox had put our vidphone screen in circuit with the tank on the bridge. Shara and McGillicuddy were studying it with rapt attention. Having nothing better to do, I did too.

McGillicuddy had been right. They *did* act more like bees, in the swarming rapidity of their movement. I couldn't get an accurate count: forty or so. And they *were* in a balloon—a faint, barely tangible thing on the fine line between transparency and translucence. Though they darted like furious red gnats, it was only within the confines of the spheroid balloon—they never left it or seemed to touch its inner surface.

As I watched, the last of the adrenalin rinsed out of my kidneys, but it left a sense of frustrated urgency. I tried to grapple with the fact that these Space Commando special effects represented something that was more important than Shara. It was a primevally disturbing notion, but I could not reject it.

In my mind were two voices, each hollering questions at the top of their lungs, each ignoring the other's questions. One yelled, *Are those things friendly? Or hostile? Or do they even use those concepts? How big are they? How far away? From where?* The other voice was less ambitious but just as loud; all it said, over and over again, was *How much longer can Shara remain in freefall without dooming herself?*

Shara's voice was full of wonder. "They're . . . they're *dancing.*"

I looked closer. If there was a pattern to the flies-on-garbage swarm they made, I couldn't detect it. "Looks random to me."

"Charlie, look. All that furious activity, and they never bump into each other or the walls of that envelope they're in. They must be in orbits as carefully choreographed as those of electrons."

"Do atoms dance?"

She gave me an odd look. "Don't they, Charlie?"

"Laser beam," McGillicuddy said.

We looked at him.

"Those things have to be plasmoids—the man I talked to said they were first spotted on radar. That means they're ionized gases of some kind—the kind of thing that used to cause UFO reports." He giggled, then caught himself. "If you could slice through that envelope with a laser, I'll bet you could deionize them pretty good—besides, that envelope has to hold their life support, whatever it is they metabolize."

I was dizzy. "Then we're not defenseless?"

"You're both talking like soldiers," Shara burst out. "I tell you they're dancing. Dancers aren't fighters."

"Come on, Shara," I barked. "Even if those things happen to be remotely like us, that's not true. Samurai, karate, kung fu—they're dance." I nodded to the screen. "All we know about these animated embers is that they travel interstellar space. That's enough to scare me."

"Charlie, look at them," she commanded.

I did.

By God, they didn't look threatening. They did, the more I watched, seem to move in a dancelike way, whirling in mad adagios just too fast for the eye to follow. Not like conventional dance—more analogous to what Shara had begun with *Mass Is a Verb*. I found myself wanting to switch to another camera for contrast of perspective, and that made my mind start to wake up at last. Two ideas surfaced, the second one necessary in order to sell Cox the first.

"How far do you suppose we are from Skyfac?" I asked McGillicuddy.

He pursed his lips. "Not far. There hasn't been much more than maneuvering acceleration. The damn things were probably attracted to Skyfac in the first place—it must be the most easily visible sign of intelligent life in this system." He grimaced. "Maybe they don't *use* planets."

I reached forward and punched the audio circuit. "Major Cox."

"Get off this circuit."

"How would you like a closer view of those things?"

"We're staying put. Now stop jiggling my elbow and get off this circuit or I'll—"

"Will you listen to me? I have four mobile cameras in space, remote control, self-contained power source and light, and better resolution than you've got. They were set up to

72

tape Shara's next dance."

He shifted gears at once. "Can you patch them into my ship?"

"I think so. But I'll have to get back to the master board in Ring One."

"No good, then. I can't tie myself to a top—what if I have to fight or run?"

"Major—how far a walk is it?"

It startled him a bit. "A mile or two, as the crow flies. But you're a groundlubber."

"I've been in free fall for most of two months. Give me a portable radar and I can ground on Phobos."

"Mmmm. You're a civilian—but dammit, I need better video. Permission granted."

Now for the first idea. "Wait—one thing more. Shara and Tom must come with me."

"Nuts. This isn't a field trip."

"Major Cox—Shara *must* return to a gravity field as quickly as possible. Ring One'll do—in fact, it'd be ideal, if we enter through the 'spoke' in the center. She can descend very slowly and acclimatize gradually, the way a diver decompresses in stages, but in reverse. McGillicuddy will have to come along to stay with her—if she passes out and falls down the tube, she could break a leg even in one-sixth gee. Besides, he's better at EVA than either of us."

He thought it over. "Go."

We went.

The trip back to Ring One was far longer than any Shara or I had ever made, but under McGillicuddy's guidance we made it with minimal maneuvering. Ring, *Champion*, and aliens formed an equiangular triangle about a mile and a half on a side. Seen in perspective, the aliens took up about as much volume as Shea Stadium. They did not pause or

73

slacken in their mad gyration, but somehow they seemed to watch us across the gap to Skyfac. I got an impression of a biologist studying the strange antics of a new species. We kept our suit radios off to avoid distraction, and it made me just a little bit more susceptible to suggestion.

I left McGillicuddy with Shara and dropped down the tube six rings at a time. Carrington was waiting for me in the reception room, with two flunkies. It was plain to see that he was scared silly and trying to cover it with anger. "God damn it, Armstead, those are my bloody cameras."

"Shut up, Carrington. If you put those cameras in the hands of the best technician available—me—and if I put their data in the hands of the best strategic mind in space—Cox— we *might* be able to save your damned factory for you. And the human race for the rest of us." I moved forward, and he got out of my way. It figured. Putting all humanity in danger might just be bad PR.

After all the practicing I'd done, it wasn't hard to direct four mobile cameras through space simultaneously by eye. The aliens ignored their approach. The Skyfac comm crew fed my signals to the *Champion* and patched me in to Cox on audio. At his direction I bracketed the balloon with the cameras, shifting POV at his command. Space Command Headquarters must have recorded the video, but I couldn't hear their conversation with Cox, for which I was grateful. I gave him slow-motion replay, close-ups, split screen— everything at my disposal. The movements of individual fireflies did not appear particularly symmetrical, but patterns began to repeat. In slow motion they looked more than ever as though they were dancing, and although I couldn't be sure, it seemed to me that they were increasing their tempo. Somehow the dramatic tension of their dance seemed to build.

And then I shifted POV to the camera which included Skyfac in the background, and my heart turned to hard vacuum and I screamed in pure primal terror—halfway between Ring One and the swarm of aliens, coming up on them slowly but inexorably, was a p-suited figure that had to be Shara.

With theatrical timing, McGillicuddy appeared in the doorway, leaning heavily on the chief engineer, his face drawn with pain. He stood on one foot, the other leg plainly broken.

"Guess I can't . . . go back to exhibition work . . . after all," he gasped. "Said . . . 'I'm sorry, Tom' . . . knew she was going to swing on me . . . wiped me out anyhow. Oh dammit, Charlie, I'm sorry." He sank into an empty chair.

Cox's voice came urgently. "What the hell is going on? Who is that?"

She *had* to be on our frequency. "Shara!" I screamed. "Get your ass back in here!"

"I can't, Charlie." Her voice was startlingly loud, and very calm. "Halfway down the tube my chest started to hurt like hell."

"Ms. Drummond," Cox rapped, "if you approach any closer to the aliens I will destroy you."

She laughed, a merry sound that froze my blood. "Bullshit, Major. You aren't about to get gay with laser beams near those things. Besides, you need me as much as you do Charlie."

"What do you mean?"

"These creatures communicate by dance. It's their equivalent of speech; it has to be a sophisticated kind of sign language, like hula."

"You can't know that."

75

"I *feel* it. I know it. Hell, how else do you communicate in airless space? Major Cox, I am the only qualified interpreter the human race has at the moment. Now will you kindly shut up so I can try to learn their 'language'?"

"I have no authority to . . ."

I said an extraordinary thing. I should have been gibbering, pleading with Shara to come back, even racing for a p-suit to *bring* her back. Instead I said, "She's right. Shut up, Cox."

"What are you trying to do?"

"Damn you, *don't waste her last effort.*"

He shut up.

Panzarella came in, shot McGillicuddy full of painkiller, and set his leg right there in the room, but I was oblivious. For over an hour I watched Shara watch the aliens. I watched them myself, in the silence of utter despair, and for the life of me I could not follow their dance. I strained my mind, trying to suck meaning from their crazy whirling, and failed. The best I could do to aid Shara was to record everything that happened, for a hypothetical posterity. Several times she cried out softly, small muffled exclamations, and I ached to call out to her in reply, but did not. With the last exclamation, she used her thrusters to bring her closer to the alien swarm, and hung there for a long time.

At last her voice came over the speaker, thick and slurred at first, as though she were talking in her sleep. "God, Charlie. Strange. So strange. I'm beginning to read them."

"How?"

"Every time I begin to understand a part of the dance, it . . . it brings us closer. Not telepathy, exactly. I just . . . know them better. Maybe it is telepathy, I don't know. By dancing what they feel, they give it enough intensity to make me understand. I'm getting about one concept in three. It's stronger up close."

Cox's voice was gentle but firm. "What have you learned, Shara?"

"That Tom and Charlie were right. They are warlike. At least, there's a flavor of arrogance to them—conviction of superiority. Their dance is a challenging, a dare. Tell Tom they *do* use planets."

"What?"

"I think at one stage of their development they're corporeal, planet-bound. Then when they have matured sufficiently, they . . . become these fireflies, like caterpillars becoming butterflies . . . and head out into space."

"Why?" from Cox.

"To find spawning grounds. They want Earth."

There was a silence lasting perhaps ten seconds. Then Cox spoke up quietly. "Back away, Shara. I'm going to see what lasers will do to them."

"No!" she cried, loud enough to make a really first-rate speaker distort.

"Shara, as Charlie pointed out to me, you are not only expendable, you are for all practical purposes expended."

"No!" This time it was me shouting.

"Major," Shara said urgently, "that's not the way. Believe me, they can dodge or withstand anything you or Earth can throw at them. I *know*."

"Hell and damnation, woman," Cox said, "what do you want me to do? Let them have the first shot? There are vessels from four countries on their way right now."

"Major, wait. Give me time."

He began to swear, then cut off. "How much time?"

She made no direct reply. "If only this telepathy thing works in reverse . . . it must. I'm no more strange to them

77

than they are to me. Probably less so; I get the idea they've been around. Charlie?"

"Yeah."

"This is a take."

I knew. I had known since I first saw her in open space on my monitor. And I knew what she needed now, from the faint trembling of her voice. It took everything I had, and I was only glad I had it to give. With extremely realistic good cheer, I said, "Break a leg, kid," and killed my mike before she could hear the sob that followed.

And she danced.

It began slowly, the equivalent of one-finger exercises, as she sought to establish a vocabulary of motion that the creatures could comprehend. *Can you see,* she seemed to say, *that* this *movement is a reaching, a yearning? Do you see that* this *is a spurning,* this *an unfolding,* that *a graduated elision of energy? Do you feel the ambiguity in the way I distort this arabesque, or that the tension can be resolved* so?

And it seemed that Shara was right, that they had infinitely more experience with disparate cultures than we, for they were superb linguists of motion. It occurred to me later that perhaps they had selected motion for communication because of its very universality. At any rate as Shara's dance began to build, their own began to slow down perceptibly in speed and intensity, until at last they hung motionless in space watching her.

Soon after that Shara must have decided that she had sufficiently defined her terms, at least well enough for pidgin communication—for now she began to dance in earnest. Before she had used only her own muscles and the shifting masses of her limbs. Now she added thrusters, singly and in combination, moving within as well as in space. Her dance became a true dance: more than a collection of motions, a thing of substance and meaning. It was unquestionably the *Stardance*, just as she had prechoreographed it, as she had always intended to dance it. That it had something to say to utterly alien creatures, of man and his nature, was not at all a coincidence: it was the essential and ultimate statement of the greatest artist of her age, and it had something to say to God himself.

The camera lights struck silver from her p-suit, gold from the twin airtanks on her shoulders. To and fro against the black backdrop of space, she wove the intricacies of her dance, a leisurely movement that seemed somehow to leave echoes behind it. And the meaning of those great loops and whirls slowly became clear, drying my throat and clamping my teeth.

For her dance spoke of nothing more and nothing less than the tragedy of being alive, and being human. It spoke, most eloquently, of pain. It spoke, most knowingly, of despair. It spoke of the cruel humor of limitless ambition yoked to limited ability, of eternal hope invested in an ephemeral lifetime, of the driving need to try and create an inexorably predetermined future. It spoke of fear, and of hunger, and, most clearly, of the basic loneliness and alienation of the human animal. It described the universe through the eyes of man: a hostile environment, the embodiment of entropy, into which we are all thrown alone, forbidden by our nature to touch another mind save secondhand, by proxy. It spoke of the blind perversity which forces man to strive hugely for a peace which, once attained, becomes boredom. And it spoke of folly, of the terrible paradox by which man is simultaneously capable of reason and unreason, forever unable to cooperate even with himself.

It spoke of Shara and her life.

Again and again, cyclical statements of hope began, only

to collapse into confusion and ruin. Again and again, cascades of energy strove for resolution, and found only frustration. All at once she launched into a pattern that seemed familiar, and in moments I recognized it: the closing movement of *Mass Is a Verb* recapitulated—not repeated but reprised, echoed, the Three Questions given a more terrible urgency by this new altar on which they were piled. And as before, it segued into that final relentless contraction, that ultimate drawing inward of all energies. Her body became derelict, abandoned, drifting in space, the essence of her being withdrawn to her center and invisible.

The quiescent aliens stirred for the first time.

And suddenly she exploded, blossoming from her contraction not as a spring uncoils, but as a flower bursts from a seed. The force of her release flung her through the void as though she were tossed like a gull in a hurricane by galactic winds. Her center appeared to hurl itself through space and time, yanking her body into a new dance.

And the new dance said, *This is what it is to be human: to see the essential existential futility of all action, all striving—and to act, to strive. This is what it is to be human: to reach forever beyond your grasp. This is what it is to be human: to live forever or die trying. This is what it is to be human: to perpetually ask the unanswerable questions, in the hope that the asking of them will somehow hasten the day when they will be answered. This is what it is to be human: to strive in the face of the certainty of failure.*

This is what it is to be human: to persist.

It said all this with a soaring series of cyclical movements that held all the rolling majesty of grand symphony, as uniquely different from each other as snowflakes, and as similar. And the new dance laughed, and it laughed as much at tomorrow as it did at yesterday, and it laughed most of all at today.

For this is what it means to be human: to laugh at what

another would call tragedy.

The aliens seemed to recoil from the ferocious energy, startled, awed, and faintly terrified by Shara's indomitable spirit. They seemed to wait for her dance to wane, for her to exhaust herself, and her laughter sounded on my speaker as she redoubled her efforts, became a pinwheel, a Catherine wheel. She changed the focus of her dance, began to dance *around* them, in pyrotechnic spatters of motion that came ever closer to the intangible spheroid which contained them. They cringed inward from her, huddling together in the center of the envelope, not so much physically threatened as cowed.

This, said her body, *is what it means to be human: to commit hara-kiri, with a smile, if it becomes needful.*

And before that terrible assurance, the aliens broke. Without warning, fireflies and balloon vanished, gone, *elsewhere.*

I know that Cox and McGillicuddy were still alive, because I saw them afterward, and that means they were probably saying and doing things in my hearing and presence, but I neither heard nor saw them then; they were as dead to me as everything except Shara. I called out her name, and she approached the camera that was lit, until I could make out her face behind the plastic hood of her p-suit.

"We may be puny, Charlie," she puffed, gasping for breath. "But by Jesus, we're tough."

"Shara—come on in now."

"You know I can't."

"Carrington'll *have* to give you a free-fall place to live now."

"A life of exile? For what? To dance? Charlie, *I haven't got anything more to say.*"

"Then I'll come out there."

"Don't be silly. Why? So you can hug a p-suit? Tenderly

81

bump hoods one last time? Balls. It's a good exit so far—let's not blow it."

"*Shara!*" I broke completely, just caved in on myself and collapsed into great racking sobs.

"Charlie, listen now," she said softly, but with an urgency that reached me even in my despair. "Listen now, for I haven't much time. I have something to give you. I hoped you'd find it for yourself, but . . . will you listen?"

"Y-yes."

"Charlie, zero-gee dance is going to get awful popular all of a sudden. I've opened the door. But you know how fads are; they'll bitch it all up unless you move fast. I'm leaving it in your hands."

"What . . . what are you talking about?"

"About you, Charlie. You're going to dance again."

Oxygen starvation, I thought. But she can't be that low on air already. "Okay. Sure thing."

"For God's sake stop humoring me—I'm straight, I tell you. You'd have seen it yourself if you weren't so damned stupid. Don't you understand? *There's nothing wrong with your leg in free fall!*"

My jaw dropped.

"Do you hear me, Charlie? You can dance again!"

"No," I said, and searched for a reason why not. "I . . . you can't . . . it's . . . dammit, the leg's not strong enough for inside work."

"Forget for the moment that inside work'll be less than half of what you do. Forget it and remember that smack in the nose you gave Carrington. Charlie, when you leaped over the desk, *you pushed off with your right leg.*"

I sputtered for a while and shut up.

"There you go, Charlie. My farewell gift. You know I've never been in love with you . . . but you must know that I've always loved you. Still do."

"I love you, Shara."

"So long, Charlie. Do it right."

And all four thrusters went off at once. I watched her go down. A while after she was too far to see, there was a long golden flame that arced above the face of the globe, waned, and then flared again as the airtanks went up.

There's a tired old hack plot about the threat of alien invasion unifying mankind overnight. It's about as realistic as Love Will Find a Way—if those damned fireflies ever come back, they'll find us just as disorganized as we were the last time. There you go.

Carrington, of course, tried to grab all the tapes and all the money—but neither Shara nor I had ever signed a contract, and her will was most explicit. So he tried to buy the judge, and he picked the wrong judge, and when it hit the papers and he saw how public and private opinion were going, he left Skyfac in a p-suit with no thrusters. I think he wanted to go the same way she had, but he was unused to EVA and let go too late. He was last seen heading in the general direction of Betelgeuse. The Skyfac board of directors picked a new man who was most anxious to wash off the stains, and he offered me continued use of all facilities.

And so I talked it over with Norrey, and she was free, and that's how the Shara Drummond Company of New Modern Dance was formed. We specialize in good dancers who couldn't cut it on Earth for one reason or another, and there are a surprising hell of a lot of them.

I enjoy dancing with Norrey. Together we're not as good as Shara was alone—but we mesh well. In spite of the obvious contraindications, I think our marriage is going to work.

That's the thing about us humans: we persist.

MELANCHOLY ELEPHANTS

This story is dedicated to Virginia Heinlein.

She sat zazen, concentrating on not concentrating, until it was time to prepare for the appointment. Sitting *seemed* to produce the usual serenity, put everything in perspective. Her hand did not tremble as she applied her make-up; tranquil features looked back at her from the mirror. She was mildly surprised, in fact, at just how calm she was, until she got out of the hotel elevator at the garage level and the mugger made his play. She killed him instead of disabling him. Which was obviously not a measured, balanced action—the official fuss and paperwork could make her late. Annoyed at herself, she stuffed the corpse under a shiny new Westinghouse roadable whose owner she knew to be in Luna, and continued on to her own car. This would have to be squared later, and it would cost. No help for it—she fought to regain at least the semblance of tranquillity as her car emerged from the garage and turned north. Nothing must interfere with this meeting, or with her role in it.

Dozens of man-years and God knows how many dollars, she thought, *funneling down to perhaps a half hour of conversation. All the effort, all the hope. Insignificant on the scale of the Great Wheel, of course . . . but when you balance it all on a half hour of talk, it's like balancing a stereo cartridge on a needlepoint. It only takes a gram or so of weight to wear out a piece of diamond. I must be harder than diamond.*

Rather than clear a window and watch Washington, D.C. roll by beneath her car, she turned on the television. She absorbed and integrated the news, on the chance that there might be some late-breaking item she could turn to her advantage in the conversation to come; none developed. Shortly the car addressed her: "Grounding, ma'am. I.D. eyeball request." When the car landed she cleared and then opened her window, presented her pass and I.D. to a Marine in dress blues, and was cleared at once. At the Marine's direction she re-opaqued the window and surrendered control of her car to the house computer, and when the car parked itself and powered down she got out without haste. A man she knew was waiting to meet her, smiling.

"Dorothy, it's good to see you again."

"Hello, Phillip. Good of you to meet me."

"You look lovely this evening."

"You're too kind." She did not chafe at the meaningless pleasantries. She needed Phil's support, or she might. But she did reflect on how many, many sentences have been worn smooth with use, rendered meaningless by centuries of repetition. It was by no means a new thought.

"If you'll come with me, he'll see you at once."

"Thank you, Phillip." She wanted to ask what the old man's mood was, but knew it would put Phil in an impossible position.

"I rather think your luck is good; the old man seems to be in excellent spirits tonight."

She smiled her thanks, and decided that if and when Phil got around to making his pass she would accept him.

The corridors through which he led her then were broad and high and long; the building dated back to a time of cheap power. Even in Washington, few others would have dared to live in such an energy-wasteful environment. The extremely spare decor reinforced the impression created by the place's very dimensions: bare space from carpet to ceiling, broken approximately every forty meters by some exquisitely simple *objet d'art* of at least a megabuck's value, appropriately displayed. An unadorned, perfect, white porcelain bowl, over a thousand years old, on a rough cherrywood pedestal. An arresting colour photograph of a snow-covered country road, silk-screened onto stretched silver foil; the time of day changed as one walked past it. A crystal globe, a meter in diameter, within which danced a hologram of the immortal Shara Drummond; since she had ceased performing before the advent of holo technology, this had to be an expensive computer reconstruction. A small sealed glassite chamber containing the first vacuum-sculpture ever made, Nakagawa's legendary Starstone. A visitor in no hurry could study an object at leisure, then walk quite a distance in undistracted contemplation before encountering another. A visitor in a hurry, like Dorothy, would not *quite* encounter peripherally astonishing stimuli often enough to get the trick of filtering them out. Each tugged at her attention, intruded on her thoughts; they were distracting both intrinsically and as a reminder of the measure of their owner's wealth. To approach this man in his own home, whether at leisure or in haste, was to be humbled. She knew the effect was intentional, and could not transcend it; this irritated her, which irritated her. She struggled for detachment. At the end of the seemingly endless corridors was an elevator. Phillip handed her into it, punched a floor button, without giving her a chance to see which one, and stepped back into the doorway. "Good luck, Dorothy."

"Thank you, Phillip. Any topics to be sure and avoid?"

"Well . . . don't bring up hemorrhoids."

"I didn't know one could."

He smiled. "Are we still on for lunch Thursday?"

"Unless you'd rather make it dinner."

One eyebrow lifted. "And breakfast?"

She appeared to consider it. "Brunch," she decided. He half-bowed and stepped back. The elevator door closed and she forgot Phillip's existence.

Sentient beings are innumerable; I vow to save them all. The deluding passions are limitless; I vow to extinguish them all. The truth is limitless; I—

The elevator door opened again, truncating the Vow of the Bodhisattva. She had not felt the elevator stop—yet she knew that she must have descended at least a hundred meters. She left the elevator. The room was larger than she had expected; nonetheless the big powered chair dominated it easily. The chair also seemed to dominate—at least visually—its occupant. A misleading impression, as he dominated all this massive home, everything in it and, to a great degree, the country in which it stood. But he did not look like much.

A scent symphony was in progress, the cinnamon passage of Bulachevski's "Childhood." It happened to be one of her personal favourites, and this encouraged her.

"Hello, Senator."

"Hello, Mrs. Martin. Welcome to my home. Forgive me for not rising."

"Of course. It was most gracious of you to receive me."

"It is my pleasure and privilege. A man my age appreciates a chance to spend time with a woman as beautiful and intelligent as yourself."

"Senator, how soon do we start talking to each other?"

He raised that part of his face which had once held an eyebrow.

"We haven't *said* anything yet that is true. You do not

stand because you cannot. Your gracious reception cost me three carefully hoarded favours and a good deal of folding cash. More than the going rate; you are seeing me reluctantly. You have at least eight mistresses that I know of, each of whom makes me look like a dull matron. I concealed a warm corpse on the way here because I dared not be late; my time is short and my business urgent. Can we begin?"

She held her breath and prayed silently. Everything she had been able to learn about the Senator told her that this was the correct way to approach him. But was it?

The mummy-like face fissured in a broad grin. "Right away. Mrs. Martin, I like you and that's the truth. My time is short, too. What do you want of me?"

"Don't you know?"

"I can make an excellent guess. I hate guessing."

"I am heavily and publicly committed to the defeat of S.4217896."

"Yes, but for all I know you might have come here to sell out."

"Oh." She tried not to show her surprise. "What makes you think that possible?"

"Your organization is large and well-financed and fairly efficient, Mrs. Martin, and there's something about it I don't understand."

"What is that?"

"Your objective. Your arguments are weak and implausible, and whenever this is pointed out to one of you, you simply keep on pushing. Many times I have seen people take a position without apparent logic to it—but I've always been able to see the logic, if I kept on looking hard enough. But as I see it, S. '896 would work to the clear and lasting advantage of the group you claim to represent, the artists. There's too much intelligence in your organization to square with your goals. So I have to wonder what you *are* working for, and why. One possibility is that you're willing to roll over on this copyright thing in exchange for whatever it is that you *really* want. Follow me?"

"Senator, I *am* working on behalf of all artists—and in a broader sense—"

He looked pained, or rather, more pained. ". . . 'for all mankind,' oh my *God*, Mrs. Martin, really now."

"I *know* you have heard that countless times, and probably said it as often." He grinned evilly. "This is one of those rare times when it happens to be true. I believe that if S. '896 does pass, our species will suffer significant trauma."

He raised a skeletal hand, tugged at his lower lip. "Now that I have ascertained where you stand, I believe I can save you a good deal of money. By concluding this audience, and seeing that the squeeze you paid for half an hour of my time is refunded pro rata."

Her heart sank, but she kept her voice even. "Without even hearing the hidden logic behind our arguments?"

"It would be pointless and cruel to make you go into your spiel, ma'am. You see, I cannot help you."

She wanted to cry out, and savagely refused herself permission. *Control,* whispered a part of her mind, while another part shouted that a man such as this did not lightly use the words "I cannot." But he *had* to be wrong. Perhaps the sentence was only a bargaining gambit . . .

No sign of the internal conflict showed; her voice was calm and measured. "Sir, I have not come here to lobby. I simply wanted to inform you personally that our organization intends to make a no-strings campaign donation in the amount of—"

"Mrs. Martin, please! Before you commit yourself, I repeat, I cannot help you. Regardless of the sum offered."

"Sir, it is substantial."

"I'm sure. Nonetheless it is insufficient."

She knew she should not ask. "Senator, *why?*"

He frowned, a frightening sight.

"Look," she said, the desperation almost showing through now, "keep the pro rata if it buys me an answer! Until I'm convinced that my mission is utterly hopeless, I must not abandon it: answering me is the quickest way to get me out of your office. Your scanners have watched me quite thoroughly, you know that I'm not abscamming you."

Still frowning, he nodded. "Very well. I cannot accept your campaign donation because I have already accepted one from another source."

Her very worst secret fear was realized. He had already taken money from the other side. The one thing any politician must do, no matter how powerful, is stay bought. It was all over.

All her panic and tension vanished, to be replaced by a sadness so great and so pervasive that for a moment she thought it might literally stop her heart.

Too late! Oh my darling, I was too late!

She realized bleakly that there were too many people in her life, too many responsibilities and entanglements. It would be at least a month before she could honourably suicide.

"—you all right, Mrs. Martin?" the old man was saying, sharp concern in his voice.

She gathered discipline around her like a familiar cloak. "Yes, sir, thank you. Thank you for speaking plainly." She stood up and smoothed her skirt. "And for your—"

"Mrs. Martin."

"—gracious hos—Yes?"

"Will you tell me your arguments? Why shouldn't I support '896?"

She blinked sharply. "You just said it would be pointless and cruel."

"If I held out the slightest hope, yes, it would be. If you'd rather not waste your time, I will not compel you. But I am curious."

"Intellectual curiosity?"

He seemed to sit up a little straighter—surely an illusion, for a prosthetic spine is not motile. "Mrs. Martin, I happen to be committed to a course of action. That does not mean I don't care whether the action is good or bad."

"Oh." She thought for a moment. "If I convince you, you will not thank me."

"I know. I saw the look on your face a moment ago, and . . . it reminded me of a night many years ago. Night my mother died. If you've got a sadness that big, and I can take on a part of it, I should try. Sit down."

She sat.

"Now tell me: what's so damned awful about extending copyright to meet the realities of modern life? Customarily I try to listen to both sides before accepting a campaign donation—but this seemed so open and shut, so straightforward . . ."

"Senator, that bill is a short-term boon, to some artists— and a long-term disaster for all artists, on Earth and off."

" 'In the long run, Mr. President—',", he began, quoting Keynes.

" '—we are some of us still alive',", she finished softly and pointedly. "Aren't we? You've put your finger on part of the problem."

"What is this disaster you speak of?" he asked.

"The worst psychic trauma the race has yet suffered."

He studied her carefully and frowned again. "Such a possibility is not even hinted at in your literature or materials."

"To do so would precipitate the trauma. At present only a handful of people know, even in my organization. I'm telling *you* because you asked, and because I am certain that you are the only person recording this conversation. I'm betting that you will wipe the tape."

He blinked, and sucked at the memory of his teeth. "My, my," he said mildly. "Let me get comfortable." He had the chair recline sharply and massage his lower limbs; she saw that he could still watch her by overhead mirror if he chose. His eyes were closed. "All right, go ahead."

She needed no time to choose her words. "Do you know how old art is, Senator?"

"As old as man, I suppose. In fact, it may be part of the definition."

"Good answer," she said. "Remember that. But for all present-day intents and purposes, you might as well say that art is a little over 15,600 years old. That's the age of the oldest surviving artwork, the cave paintings at Lascaux. Doubtless the cave-painters sang, and danced, and even told stories— but these arts left no record more durable than the memory of a man. Perhaps it was the story tellers who next learned how to preserve their art. Countless more generations would pass before a workable method of musical notation was devised and standardized. Dancers only learned in the last few centuries how to leave even the most rudimentary record of their art.

"The racial memory of our species has been getting longer since Lascaux. The biggest single improvement came with the invention of writing: our memory-span went from a few generations to as many as the Bible has been around. But it took a massive effort to sustain a memory that long: it was difficult to hand-copy manuscripts faster than barbarians, plagues, or other natural disasters could destroy them. The obvious solution was the printing press: to make and disseminate so many copies of a manuscript or artwork that *some* would survive any catastrophe.

"But with the printing press a new idea was born. Art was suddenly mass-marketable, and there was money in it. Writers decided that they should own the right to copy their work. The notion of copyright was waiting to be born.

"Then in the last hundred and fifty years came the largest quantum jumps in human racial memory. Recording technologies. Visual: photography, film, video, Xerox, holo. Audio: low-fi, hi-fi, stereo, and digital. Then computers, the ultimate in information storage. Each of these technologies generated new art forms, and new ways of preserving the ancient art forms. And each required a reassessment of the idea of copyright.

"You know the system we have now, unchanged since the mid-twentieth-century. Copyright ceases to exist fifty years after the death of the copyright holder. But the size of the human race has increased drastically since the 1900s—and so has the average human lifespan. Most people in developed nations now expect to live to be a hundred and twenty; you yourself are considerably older. And so, naturally, S. '896 now seeks to extend copyright into perpetuity."

"Well," the senator interrupted, "what is *wrong* with that? Should a man's work cease to be his simply because he has neglected to keep on breathing? Mrs. Martin, you yourself will be wealthy all your life if that bill passes. Do you truly wish to give away your late husband's genius?"

She winced in spite of herself.

"Forgive my bluntness, but that is what I understand *least* about your position."

"Senator, if I try to hoard the fruits of my husband's genius, I may cripple my race. Don't you see what perpetual copyright implies? It is perpetual racial memory! That bill will give the human race an elephant's memory. *Have you ever seen a cheerful elephant?*"

He was silent for a time. Then: "I'm still not sure I understand the problem."

"Don't feel bad, sir. The problem has been directly under the nose of all of us for at *least* eighty years, and hardly anyone has noticed."

"Why is that?"

"I think it comes down to a kind of innate failure of mathematical intuition, common to most humans. We tend to confuse any sufficiently high number with infinity."

"Well, anything above ten to the eighty-fifth might as well be infinity."

"Beg pardon?"

"Sorry—I should not have interrupted. That is the current best-guess for the number of atoms in the Universe. Go on."

She struggled to get back on the rails. "Well, it takes a lot less than that to equal 'infinity' in most minds. For millions of years we looked at the ocean and said, 'That is infinite. It will accept our garbage and waste forever.' We looked at the sky and said, 'That is infinite: it will hold an infinite amount of smoke.' We *like* the idea of infinity. A problem with infinity in it is easily solved. How long can you pollute a planet infinitely large? Easy: forever. Stop thinking.

"Then one day there are so many of us that the planet no longer seems infinitely large.

"So we go elsewhere. There are infinite resources in the *rest* of the solar system, aren't there? I think you are one of the few people alive wise enough to realize that there are *not* infinite resources in the solar system, and sophisticated enough to have included that awareness in your plans."

The Senator now looked troubled. He sipped something from a straw. "Relate all this to your problem."

"Do you remember a case from about eighty years ago, involving the song 'My Sweet Lord,' by George Harrison?"

"Remember it? I did research on it. My firm won."

"Your firm convinced the court that Harrison had gotten the tune for that song from a song called 'He's So Fine,' written over ten years earlier. Shortly thereafter Yoko Ono was accused of stealing 'You're My Angel' from the classic 'Makin' Whoopee,' written more than thirty years earlier. Chuck Berry's estate eventually took John Lennon's estate to court over 'Come Together.' Then in the late '80s the great Plagiarism Plague *really* got started in the courts. From then on it was open season on popular composers, and still is. But it really hit the fan at the turn of the century, when Brindle's *Ringsong* was shown to be 'substantially similar' to one of Corelli's concertos.

"There are eighty-eight notes. One hundred and seventy-six, if your ear is good enough to pick out quarter tones. Add in rests and so forth, different time signatures. Pick a figure for maximum number of notes a melody can contain. I do not know the figure for the maximum possible number of melodies—too many variables—but I am sure it is quite high.

"I am certain that is not infinity.

"For one thing, a great many of those possible arrays of eighty-eight notes will not be perceived as music, as melody, by the human ear. Perhaps more than half. They will not be hummable, whistleable, listenable—some will be actively unpleasant to hear. Another large fraction will be so similar to each other as to be effectively identical: if you change three notes of the Moonlight Sonata, you have not created something new.

"I do not know the figure for the maximum number of discretely appreciable melodies, and again I'm certain it is quite high, and again I am certain that it is not infinity. There are sixteen billion of us alive, Senator, more than all the people that have ever lived. Thanks to our technology, better than half of us have no meaningful work to do; fifty-four percent of our population is entered on the tax rolls as artists. Because the synthesizer is so cheap and versatile, a majority of those artists are musicians, and a great many are composers. Do you know what it is like to be a composer these days, Senator?"

"I know a few composers."

"Who are still working?"

"Well . . . three of 'em."

"How often do they bring out a new piece?"

Pause. "I would say once every five years on the average. Hmmm. Never thought of it before, but—"

"Did you know that at present two out of every five copyright submissions to the Music Division are rejected on the first computer search?"

The old man's face had stopped registering surprise, other than for histrionic purposes, more than a century before; nonetheless, she knew she had rocked him. "No, I did not."

"Why would you know? Who would talk about it? But it is a fact nonetheless. Another fact is that, when the increase in number of working composers is taken into account, the *rate* of submissions to the Copyright Office is decreasing significantly. There are more composers than ever, but their individual productivity is declining. Who is the most popular composer alive?"

"Uh . . . I suppose that Vachandra fellow."

"Correct. He has been working for a little over fifty years. If you began now to play every note he ever wrote, in succession, you would be done in twelve hours. Wagner wrote well over sixty hours of music—the Ring alone runs twenty-one hours. The Beatles—essentially two composers—produced over twelve hours of original music in *less than ten years*. Why were the greats of yesteryear so much more prolific?

"There were more enjoyable permutations of eighty-eight notes for them to find."

"Oh my," the Senator whispered.

"Now go back to the 1970s again. Remember the *Roots* plagiarism case? And the dozens like it that followed? Around the same time a writer named van Vogt sued the makers of a successful film called *Alien*, for plagiarism of a story forty years later. Two other writers named Bova and Ellison sued a television studio for stealing a series idea. All three collected.

"That ended the legal principle that one does not copyright *ideas* but *arrangements of words*. The number of word arrangements is finite, but the number of *ideas* is *much* smaller. Certainly, they can be retold in endless ways—*West Side Story* is a brilliant reworking of *Romeo and Juliet*. But it was only possible because *Romeo and Juliet* was in the public domain. Remember too that of the finite number of stories that can be told, a certain number will be *bad stories*.

"As for visual artists—well, once a man demonstrated in the laboratory an ability to distinguish between eighty-one distinct shades of colour accurately. I think that's an upper limit. There is a maximum amount of information that the eye is capable of absorbing, and much of that will be the equivalent of noise—"

"But . . . but . . ." This man was reputed never to have hesitated in any way under any circumstances. "But there'll always be change . . . there'll always be new discoveries, new horizons, new social attitudes, to infuse art with new—"

"Not as fast as artists breed. Do you know about the great

split in literature at the beginning of the twentieth century? The mainstream essentially abandoned the Novel of Ideas after Henry James, and turned its collective attention to the Novel of Character. They had sucked that dry by mid-century, and they're still chewing on the pulp today. Meanwhile a small group of writers, desperate for something new to write about, for a new story to tell, invented a new genre called science fiction. They mined the future for ideas. The infinite future—like the infinite coal and oil and copper they had then too. In less than a century they had mined it out; there hasn't been a genuinely original idea in science fiction in over fifty years. Fantasy has always been touted as the 'literature of infinite possibility'—but there is even a theoretical upper limit to the 'meaningfully impossible,' and we are fast reaching it."

"We can create new art forms," he said.

"People have been trying to create new art forms for a long time, sir. Almost all fell by the wayside. People just didn't like them."

"We'll *learn* to like them. Damn it, we'll have to."

"And they'll help, for a while. More new art forms have been born in the last two centuries than in the previous million years—though none in the last fifteen years. Scent-symphonies, tactile sculpture, kinetic sculpture, zero-gravity dance—they're all rich new fields, and they are generating mountains of new copyrights. Mountains of finite size. The ultimate bottleneck is this: that *we have only five senses with which to apprehend art, and that is a finite number.* Can I have some water, please?"

"Of course."

The old man appeared to have regained his usual control, but the glass which emerged from the arm of her chair contained apple juice. She ignored this and continued.

"But that's not what I'm afraid of, Senator. The theoretical heat-death of artistic expression is something we may never really approach in fact. Long before that point, the game will collapse."

She paused to gather her thoughts, sipped her juice. A part of her mind noted that it harmonized with the recurrent cinnamon motif of Bulachevski's scent-symphony, which was still in progress.

"Artists have been deluding themselves for centuries with the notion that they create. In fact they do nothing of the sort. They discover. Inherent in the nature of reality are a number of combinations of musical tones that will be perceived as pleasing by a human central nervous system. For millennia we have been discovering them, implicit in the universe—and telling ourselves that we 'created' them. To create implies infinite possibility, to discover implies finite possibility. As a species I think we will react poorly to having our noses rubbed in the fact that we are discoverers and not creators."

She stopped speaking and sat very straight. Unaccountably her feet hurt. She closed her eyes, and continued speaking.

"My husband wrote a song for me, on the occasion of our fortieth wedding anniversary. It was our love in music, unique and special and intimate, the most beautiful melody I ever heard in my life. It made him so happy to have written it. Of his last ten compositions he had burned five for being derivative, and the others had all failed copyright clearance. But this was fresh, special—he joked that my love for him had inspired him. The next day he submitted it for clearance, and learned that it had been a popular air during his early childhood, and had already been unsuccessfully submitted fourteen times since its original registration. A week later he burned all his manuscripts and working tapes and killed himself."

She was silent for a long time, and the Senator did not speak.

" 'Ars longa, vita brevis est,' " she said at last. "There's been comfort of a kind in that for thousands of years. But art is long, not infinite. 'The Magic goes away.' One day we will *use it up*—unless we can learn to recycle it like any other finite resource." Her voice gained strength. "Senator, that bill has to fail, if I have to take you on to do it. Perhaps I can't win—but I'm going to fight you! A copyright must not be allowed to last more than fifty years—after which it should be flushed from the memory banks of the Copyright Office. We need selective voluntary amnesia if Discoverers of Art are to continue to work without psychic damage. Facts should be remembered—but dreams?" She shivered. ". . . Dreams should be forgotten when we wake. Or one day we will find ourselves unable to sleep. Given eight billion artists with effective working lifetimes in excess of a century, we can no longer allow individuals to own their discoveries in perpetuity. We must do it the way the human race did it for a million years—by forgetting, and rediscovering. Because one day the infinite number of monkeys will have nothing else to write *except* the complete works of Shakespeare. And they would probably rather not *know* that when it happens."

Now she was finished, nothing more to say. So was the scent-symphony, whose last motif was fading slowly from the air. No clock ticked, no artifact hummed. The stillness was complete, for perhaps half a minute.

"If you live long enough," the Senator said slowly at last, "there is nothing new under the sun." He shifted in his great chair. "If you're lucky, you die sooner than that. I haven't heard a new dirty joke in fifty years." He seemed to sit up straight in his chair. "I will kill S.4217896."

She stiffened in shock. After a time, she slumped slightly

and resumed breathing. So many emotions fought for ascendancy that she barely had time to recognize them as they went by. She could not speak.

"Furthermore," he went on, "I will not tell anyone why I'm doing it. It will begin the end of my career in public life, which I did not ever plan to leave, but you have convinced me that I must. I am both . . . glad, and—" His face tightened with pain. "—and *bitterly* sorry that you told me why I must."

"So am I, sir," she said softly, almost inaudibly.

He looked at her sharply. "Some kinds of fights, you can't feel good even if you win them. Only two kinds of people take on fights like that: fools, and remarkable people. I think you are a remarkable person, Mrs. Martin."

She stood, knocking over her juice. "I wish to God I were a fool," she cried, feeling her control begin to crack at last.

"Dorothy!" he thundered.

She flinched as if he had struck her. "Sir?" she said automatically.

"Do *not* go to pieces! That is an order. You're wound up too tight; the pieces might not go back together again."

"So what?" she asked bitterly.

He was using the full power of his voice now, the voice which had stopped at least one war. "So how many friends do you think a man my age has *got*, damn it? Do you think minds like yours are common? We *share* this business now, and that makes us friends. You are the first person to come out of that elevator and really surprise me in a quarter of a century. And soon, when the word gets around that I've broken faith, people will stop coming out of the elevator. You think like me, and I can't afford to lose you." He smiled, and the smile seemed to melt decades from his face. "Hang on, Dorothy," he said, "and we will comfort each other in our terrible knowledge. All right?"

For several moments she concentrated exclusively on her breathing, slowing and regularizing it. Then, tentatively, she probed at her emotions.

"Why," she said wonderingly, "it *is* better . . . shared."

"Anything is."

She looked at him then, and tried to smile and finally succeeded. "Thank you, Senator."

He returned her smile as he wiped all recordings of their conversation. "Call me Bob."

"Yes, Robert."

GOD IS AN IRON

I smelled her before I saw her. Even so, the first sight was shocking.

She was sitting in a tan plastic-surfaced armchair, the kind where the front comes up as the back goes down. It was back as far as it would go. It was placed beside the large living room window, which was transparent. A plastic block table next to it held a digital clock, a dozen unopened packages of self-lighting Peter Jackson cigarettes, an empty ashtray, a full vial of cocaine, and a lamp with a bulb of at least a hundred and fifty watts. It illuminated her with brutal clarity.

She was naked. Her skin was the color of vanilla pudding. Her hair was in rats, her nails unpainted and untended, some overlong and some broken. There was dust on her. She sat in a ghastly sludge of feces and urine.

Dried vomit was caked on her chin and between her breasts and down her ribs to the chair.

These were only part of what I had smelled. The predominant odor was of fresh-baked bread. It is the smell of a person who is starving to death. The combined effluvia had prepared me to find a senior citizen, paralyzed by a stroke or some such crisis.

I judged her to be about twenty-five years old.

I moved to where she could see me, and she did not see

me. That was probably just as well, because I had just seen the two most horrible things. The first was the smile. They say that when the bomb went off at Hiroshima, some people's shadows were baked onto walls by it. I think that smile got baked on the surface of my brain in much the same way. I don't want to talk about that smile.

The second horrible thing was the one that explained all the rest. From where I now stood, I could see a triple socket in the wall beneath the window. Into it were plugged the lamp, the clock, and her.

I knew about wireheading, of course—I had lost a couple of acquaintances and one friend to the juice. But I had never *seen* a wirehead. It is by definition a solitary vice, and all the public usually gets to see is a sheeted figure being carried out to the wagon.

The transformer lay on the floor beside the chair, where it had been dropped. The switch was on, and the timer had been jiggered so that instead of providing one five- or ten- or fifteen-second jolt per hour, it allowed continuous flow. That timer is required by law on all juice rigs sold, and you need special tools to defeat it. Say, a nail file. The input cord was long, and fell in crazy coils from the wall socket. The output cord disappeared beneath the chair, but I knew where it ended. It ended in the tangled snarl of her hair, at the crown of her head, in a miniplug. The plug was snapped into a jack surgically implanted in her skull, and from the jack tiny wires snaked their way through the wet jelly to the hypothalamus, to the specific place in the medial forebrain bundle where the major pleasure center of her brain was located. She had sat there in total transcendent ecstasy for at least five days.

I moved finally. I moved closer, which surprised me.

She saw me now, and impossibly the smile became a bit wider. I was marvelous. I was captivating. I was her perfect lover. I could not look at the smile; a small plastic tube ran from one corner of the smile and my eyes followed it gratefully. It was held in place by small bits of surgical tape at her jaw, neck, and shoulder, and from there it ran in a lazy curve to the big fifty-liter water cooler bottle on the floor. She had plainly meant her suicide to last: she had arranged to die of hunger rather than thirst, which would have been quicker. She could take a drink when she happened to think of it; and if she forgot, well, what the hell.

My intention must have shown on my face, and I think she even understood it—the smile began to fade. That decided me. I moved before she could force her neglected body to react, whipped the plug out of the wall, and stepped back warily.

Her body did not go rigid as if galvanized. It had already been so for many days. What it did was the exact opposite, and the effect was just as striking. She seemed to shrink. Her eyes slammed shut. She slumped. Well, I thought, it'll be a long day and a night before *she* can move a voluntary muscle again, and then she hit me before I knew she had left the chair, breaking my nose with the heel of one fist and bouncing the other off the side of my head. We cannoned off each other and I managed to keep my feet; she whirled and grabbed the lamp. Its cord was stapled to the floor and would not yield, so she set her feet and yanked and it snapped off clean at the base. In near-total darkness she raised the lamp on high and came at me and I lunged inside the arc of her swing and punched her in the solar plexus. She said *guff!* and went down.

I staggered to a couch and sat down and felt my nose and fainted.

I don't think I was out very long. The blood tasted fresh.

I woke with a sense of terrible urgency. It took me a while

to work out why. When someone has been simultaneously starved and unceasingly stimulated for days on end, it is not the best idea in the world to depress their respiratory center. I lurched to my feet.

It was not completely dark, there was a moon somewhere out there. She lay on her back, arms at her sides, perfectly relaxed. Her ribs rose and fell in great slow swells. A pulse showed strongly at her throat. As I knelt beside her she began to snore, deeply and rhythmically.

I had time for second thoughts now. It seemed incredible that my impulsive action had not killed her. Perhaps that had been my subconscious intent. Five days of wireheading alone should have killed her, never mind sudden cold turkey.

I probed in the tangle of hair, found the empty jack. The hair around it was dry. If she hadn't torn the skin in yanking herself loose, it was unlikely that she had sustained any more serious damage within. I continued probing, found no soft places on the skull. Her forehead felt cool and sticky to my hand. The fecal smell was overpowering the baking bread now.

There was no pain in my nose yet, but it felt immense and pulsing. I did not want to touch it, or to think about it. My shirt was soaked with blood; I wiped my face with it and tossed it into a corner. It took everything I had to lift her. She was unreasonably heavy, and I say that having carried drunks and corpses. There was a hall off the living room, and all halls lead to a bathroom. I headed that way in a clumsy staggering trot, and just as I reached the deeper darkness, with my pulse at its maximum, my nose woke up and began screaming. I nearly dropped her then and clapped my hands to my face; the temptation was overwhelming. Instead I whimpered like a dog and kept going. Childhood feeling: runny nose you can't wipe. At each door I came to, I teetered on one leg and kicked it open, and the third one gave the right small-room, acoustic-tile echo. The light switch was where they almost always are; I rubbed it on with my shoulder and the room flooded with light.

Large aquamarine tub, Styrofoam recliner pillow at the head end, nonslip bottom. Aquamarine sink with ornate handles, cluttered with toiletries and cigarette butts and broken shards of mirror from the medicine cabinet above. Aquamarine commode, lid up and seat down. Brown throw rug, expensive. Scale shoved back into a corner, covered with dust in which two footprints showed. I made a massive effort and managed to set her reasonably gently in the tub. I rinsed my face and hands of blood at the sink, ignoring the broken glass, and stuffed the bleeding nostril with toilet paper. I adjusted her head, fixed the chin strap. I held both feet away from the faucet until I had the water adjusted, and then left with one hand on my nose and the other beating against my hip, in search of her liquor.

There was plenty to choose from. I found some Metaxa in the kitchen. I took great care not to bring it near my nose, sneaking it up on my mouth from below. It tasted like burning lighter fluid, and made sweat spring out on my forehead. I found a roll of paper towels, and on my way back to the bathroom I used a great wad of them to swab most of the sludge off the chair and rug. There was a growing pool of water siphoning from the plastic tube, and I stopped that. When I got back to the bathroom the water was lapping over her bloated belly, and horrible tendrils were weaving up from beneath her. It took three rinses before I was satisfied with the body. I found a hose-and-spray under the sink that mated with the tub's faucet, and that made the hair easy.

I had to dry her there in the tub. There was only one towel left, none too clean. I found a first-aid spray that incorporated a good topical anesthetic, and put it on the sores on her back and butt. I had located her bedroom on the way to the Metaxa. Wet hair slapped my arm as I carried her there. She seemed even heavier, as though she had become waterlogged. I eased the door shut behind me and tried the light-switch trick again, and it wasn't there. I moved forward into a foot-locker and lost her and went down amid multiple crashes, putting all my attention into guarding my nose. She made no sound at all, not even a grunt.

The light switch turned out to be a pull-chain over the bed. She was on her side, still breathing slow and deep. I wanted to punt her up onto the bed. My nose was a blossom of pain. I nearly couldn't lift her the third time. I was moaning with frustration by the time I had her on her left side on the king-size mattress. It was a big brass four-poster bed, with satin sheets and pillow cases, all dirty. The blankets were shoved to the bottom. I checked her skull and pulse again, peeled up each eyelid, and found uniform pupils. Her fore-head and cheek still felt cool, so I covered her. Then I kicked the footlocker clear into the corner, turned out the light, and left her snoring like a chain saw.

Her vital papers and documents were in her study, locked in a strongbox on the closet shelf. It was an expensive box, quite sturdy and proof against anything short of nuclear explosion. It had a combination lock with all of twenty-seven possible combinations. It was stuffed with papers. I laid her life out on her desk like a losing hand of solitaire, and studied it with a growing frustration.

Her name was Karen Scholz, but she used the name Karyn Shaw, which I thought phony. She was twenty-two. Divorced her parents at fourteen, uncontested no-fault. Since then she had been, at various times, waitress, secretary to a lamp salesman, painter, freelance typist, motorcycle mechanic and unlicensed masseuse. The most recent paycheck stub was from The Hard Corps, a massage parlor with a cut-rate reputation. It was dated almost a year ago. Her bank balance combined with paraphernalia I had found in the closet to tell me that she was currently self-employed as a tootlegger, a cocaine dealer. The richness of the apartment and furnishings told me that she was a foolish one. Even if the narcs missed her, very shortly the IRS was going to come down on her like a ton of bricks. Perhaps subconsciously she had not expected to be around.

Nothing there; I kept digging. She had attended community college for one semester as an art major, and dropped out failing. She had defaulted on a lease three years ago. She had wrecked a car once, and been shafted by her insurance company. Trivia. Only one major trauma in recent years: a year and a half ago she had contracted out as host-mother to a couple named Lombard/Smyth. It was a pretty good fee—she had good hips and the right rare blood type—but six months into the pregnancy they had caught her using tobacco and canceled the contract. She fought, but they had photographs. And better lawyers, naturally. She had to repay the advance, and pay for the abortion, of course, and she got socked for court costs besides.

It didn't make sense. To show clean lungs at the physical, she had to have been off cigarettes for at least three to six months. Why backslide, with so much at stake? Like the minor traumas, it felt more like an effect than a cause. Self-destructive behavior. I kept looking.

Near the bottom I found something that looked promising. Both her parents had been killed in a car smash when she was eighteen. Their obituary was paperclipped to her father's will. That will was one of the most extraordinary documents I have ever read. I could understand an angry father cutting off his only child without a dime. But what he had done was worse. He had left all his money to the church, and to her "a hundred dollars, the going rate."

Damn it, that didn't work either. So-there suicides don't wait four years. And they don't use such a garish method either; it devalues the tragedy. I decided it had to be either a very big and dangerous coke deal gone bad, or a very reptilian lover. No, not a coke deal. They would never have left her in her own apartment to die the way she wanted to. It could not be murder: even the most unscrupulous wire surgeon needs an awake, consenting subject to place the wire correctly.

A lover, then. I was relieved, pleased with my sagacity, and irritated as hell. I didn't know why. I chalked it up to my nose. It felt as though a large shark with rubber teeth was rhythmically biting it as hard as he could. I shoveled the papers back into the box, locked and replaced it, and went to the bathroom.

Her medicine cabinet would have impressed a pharmacist. She had lots of allergies. It took me five minutes to find aspirin. I took four. I picked the largest shard of mirror out of the sink, propped it on the toilet tank, and sat down backward on the seat. My nose was visibly displaced to the right, and the swelling was just hitting its stride. I removed the toilet-tissue plug from my nostril, and it resumed bleeding. There was a box of Kleenex on the floor. I ripped it apart, took out all the tissues, and stuffed them into my mouth. Then I grabbed my nose with my right hand and tugged out and to the left, simultaneously flushing the toilet with my left hand. The flushing coincided with the scream, and my front teeth met through the Kleenex. When I could see again, the nose looked straight and my breathing was unimpaired. When the bleeding stopped again I gingerly washed my face and hands and left.

A moment later I returned; something had caught my eye. It was the glass and toothbrush holder. There was only one toothbrush in it. I looked through the medicine chest again, and noticed this time that there was no shaving cream, no razor, no masculine toiletries of any kind. All the prescriptions were in her name.

I went thoughtfully to the kitchen, mixed myself a Preacher's Downfall by moonlight, and took it to her bedroom. The bedside clock said five. I lit a match, moved the footlocker in front of an armchair, sat down, and put my feet up. I sipped my drink and listened to her snore and watched her breathe in the feeble light of the clock. I decided to run through all the possibilities, and as I was formulating the first one, daylight smacked me hard in the nose.

My hands went up reflexively and I poured my drink on my head and hurt my nose more. I wake up hard in the best of times. She was still snoring. I nearly threw the empty glass at her.

It was just past noon, now; light came strongly through the heavy curtains, illuminating so much mess and disorder that I could not decide whether she had trashed her bedroom herself or it had been tossed by a pro. I finally settled on the former: the armchair I'd slept on was intact. Or had the pro found what he wanted before he got that far?

I gave it up and went to make myself breakfast. The milk was bad, of course, but I found a tolerable egg and the makings of an omelet. I don't care for black coffee, but Javanese brewed from frozen beans needs no augmentation. I drank three cups.

It took me an hour or two to clean up and air out the living room. The cord and transformer went down the oubliette, along with most of the perished items from the fridge. The dishes took three full cycles for each load, a couple of hours all told. I passed the time vacuuming and dusting and snooping, learning nothing more of significance.

The phone rang. She had no answering program in circuit, of course. I energized the screen. It was a young man in a business tunic, wearing the doggedly amiable look of the stranger who wants you to accept the call anyway. After some thought I did accept, audio-only, and let him speak first. He wanted to sell us a marvelous building lot in Forest Acres, South Dakota. I was making up a shopping list about fifteen minutes later when I heard her moan. I reached her bedroom door in seconds, waited in the doorway with both hands in sight, and said slowly and clearly, "My name is Joseph Templeton, Karen. I am a friend. You are all right now."

Her eyes were those of a small, tormented animal.

"Please don't try to get up. Your muscles won't work properly and you may hurt yourself."

No answer.

"Karen, are you hungry?"

"Your voice is ugly," she said despairingly, and her own voice was so hoarse I winced. "*My* voice is ugly," she added, and sobbed gently. "It's *all* ugly." She screwed her eyes shut.

She was clearly incapable of movement. I told her I would be right back, and went to the kitchen. I made up a tray of clear strong broth, unbuttered toast, tea with maltose, and saltine crackers. She was staring at the ceiling when I got back, and apparently it was vile. I put the tray down, lifted her, and made a backrest of pillows.

"I want a drink."

"After you eat," I said agreeably.

"Who're you?"

"Mother Templeton. Eat."

"The soup, maybe. Not the toast." She got about half of it down, did nibble at the toast, accepted some tea. I didn't want to overfill her. "My drink."

"Sure thing." I took the tray back to the kitchen, finished my shopping list, put away the last of the dishes, and put a frozen meal into the oven for my lunch. When I got back she was fast asleep.

Emaciation was near total; except for breasts and bloated belly, she was all bone and taut skin. Her pulse was steady. At her best she would not have been very attractive by conventional standards. Passable. Too much waist, not enough neck, upper legs a bit too thick for the rest of her. It's hard to evaluate a starved and unconscious face, but her jaw was a bit too square, her nose a trifle hooked, her blue eyes just the least little bit too far apart. Animated, the face might have been beautiful—any set of features can support beauty—but even a superb makeup job could not have made her pretty. There was an old bruise on her chin, another on her left hip. Her hair was sandy blonde, long and thin; it had dried in snarls that would take hours to comb out. Her breasts were magnificent, and that saddened me. In this world, a woman whose breasts are her best feature is in for a rough time.

I was putting together a picture of a life that would have depressed anyone with the sensitivity of a rhino. Back when I had first seen her, when her features were alive, she had looked sensitive. Or had that been a trick of the juice? Impossible to say now.

But damn it all to hell, I could find nothing to really explain the socket in her skull. You can hear worse life stories in any bar, on any street corner. Wireheads are usually addictive personalities, who decide at last to skip the small shit. There were no tracks on her anywhere, no nasal damage, no sign that she used any of the coke she sold. Her work history, pitiful and fragmented as it was, was too steady for any kind of serious jones; she had undeniably been hitting the sauce hard lately, but only lately. Tobacco seemed to be her only serious addiction.

That left the hypothetical bastard lover. I worried at that for a while to see if I could make it fit. To have done so much psychic damage, he would almost have to have lived with her . . . but where was his spoor?

At that point I went to the bathroom, and that settled it. When I lifted the seat to urinate, I found written on the underside with magic marker: "It's so nice to have a man around the house!" The handwriting was hers. She had lived alone.

I was relieved, because I hadn't relished thinking about my hypothetical monster or the necessity of tracking and killing him. But I was irritated as hell again.

I wanted to *understand*.

For something to do, I took my steak and a mug of coffee to the study and heated up her terminal. I tried all the typical access codes, her birthdate and her name in numbers and such, but none of them would unlock it. Then on a hunch I tried the date of her parents' death, and that did it. I ordered the groceries she needed, instructed the lobby door to accept delivery, and tried everything I could think of to get a diary or a journal out of the damned thing, without success. So I punched up the public library and asked the catalog for *Britannica* on wireheading. It referred me to brain-reward, autostimulus of. I skipped over the history, from discovery by Olds and others in 1956 to emergence as a social problem in the late nineties, when surgery got simple; declined the offered diagrams, graphs, and technical specs; finally found a brief section on motivations.

There was indeed one type of typical user I had overlooked. The terminally ill.

Could that really be it? At her age? I went to the bathroom and checked the prescriptions. Nothing for heavy pain, nothing indicating anything more serious than allergies. Back before telephones had cameras I might have conned something out of her personal physician, but it would have been a chancy thing even then. There was no way to test the hypothesis.

It was possible, even plausible—but it just wasn't *likely* enough to satisfy the thing inside me that demanded an explanation. I dialed a game of four-wall squash, and made sure the computer would let me win. I was almost enjoying myself when she screamed.

It wasn't much of a scream; her throat was shot. But it fetched me at once. I saw the problem as I cleared the door. The topical anesthetic had worn off the large sores on her back and buttocks, and the pain had woken her. Now that I thought about it, it should have happened earlier; that spray was only supposed to be good for a few hours. I decided that her pleasure-pain system was weakened by overload.

The sores were bad; she would have scars. I resprayed them, and her moans stopped nearly at once. I could devise no means of securing her on her belly that would not be nightmare inducing, and decided it was unnecessary. I thought she was out again, and started to leave. Her voice, muffled by pillows, stopped me in my tracks.

"I don't know you. Maybe you're not even real. I can tell you."

"Save your energy, Karen. You—"

"Shut up. You wanted the karma, you got it."

I shut up.

Her voice was flat, dead. "All my friends were dating at

twelve. *He* made me wait until fourteen. Said I couldn't be trusted. Tommy came to take me to the dance, and he gave Tommy a hard time. I was so embarrassed. The dance was nice for a couple of hours. Then Tommy started chasing after Jo Tompkins. He just left me and went off with her. I went into the ladies' room and cried for a long time. A couple of girls got the story out of me, and one of them had a bottle of vodka in her purse. I never drank before.

"When I started tearing up cars in the parking lot, one of the girls got ahold of Tommy. She gave him shit and made him take me home. I don't remember it, I found out later—"

Her throat gave out and I got water. She accepted it without meeting my eyes, turned her face away and continued.

"Tommy got me in the door somehow. I was out cold by then. He'd been fooling around with me a little in the car, I think. He must have been too scared to try and get me upstairs. He left me on the couch and my underpants on the rug and went home. The next thing I knew, I was on the floor and my face hurt. *He* was standing over me. *Whore* he said. I got up and tried to explain and he hit me a couple of times. I ran for the door but he hit me hard in the back. I went into the stairs and banged my head real hard."

Feeling began to come into her voice for the first time. The feeling was fear. I dared not move.

"When I woke up it was day. Mama must have bandaged my head and put me to bed. My head hurt a lot. When I came out of the bathroom I heard him call me. Him and Mama were in bed. He started in on me. Wouldn't let me talk, and he kept getting madder and madder. Finally I hollered back at him. He got up off the bed and started in hitting me again. My robe came off. He kept hitting me in the belly and tits, and his fists were like hammers. *Slut,* he kept saying. *Whore.* I thought he was going to kill me so I grabbed one arm and bit. He roared like a dragon and threw me across the room. Onto the bed. Mama jumped up. Then he pulled down his underpants and it was big and purple. I screamed and screamed and tore at his back and Mama just stood there. Her eyes were big and round, just like in cartoons. His breath stank and I screamed and screamed and—"

She broke off short and her shoulders knotted. When she continued, her voice was stone dead again. "I woke up in my own bed again. I took a real long shower and went downstairs. Mama was making pancakes. I sat down and she gave me one and I ate it, and then I threw it up right there on the table and ran out the door. She never said a word, never called me back. After school that day I found a Sanctuary and started the divorce proceedings. I never saw either of them again. I never told this to anybody before."

The pause was so long I thought she had fallen asleep. "Since that time I've tried it with men and women and boys and girls, in the dark and in the desert sun, with people I cared for and people I didn't give a damn about, and I have never understood the pleasure in it. The best it's ever been for me is not uncomfortable. God, how I've wondered . . . well, now I know." She was starting to drift. "Only thing my whole life turned out *better* 'n cracked up to be." She snorted sleepily. "Even alone."

I sat there for a long time without moving. My legs trembled when I got up, and my hands trembled while I made supper.

That was the last time she was lucid for nearly forty-eight hours. I plied her with successively stronger soups every time she woke up, and once I got a couple of pieces of tea-soggy toast into her. Sometimes she called me by others' names, and sometimes she didn't know I was there, and everything she said was disjointed. I listened to her tapes and CDs, watched some of her videos, charged some books and games to her computer account. I took a lot of her aspirin. And drank surprisingly little of her booze.

It was frustrating. I still couldn't make it all fit together. There was a large piece missing. The animal who sired and raised her had planted the charge, of course, and I perceived that it was big enough to blow her apart. But why had it taken eight years to go off? If his death four years ago had not triggered it, what had? I could not leave until I knew.

Midway through the second day her plumbing started working again; I had to change the sheets. The next morning a noise woke me and I found her on the bathroom floor on her knees in a pool of urine. I got her clean and back to bed, and just as I thought she was going to drift off she started yelling at me. "Lousy son of a bitch, it could have been over! I'll never have the guts again now! How could you *do* that, you *bastard,* it was so *nice!*" She turned violently away from me and curled up. I had to make a hard choice then, and I gambled on what I knew of loneliness and sat on the edge of the bed and stroked her hair as gently and impersonally as I knew how. It was a good guess. She began to cry, in great racking heaves first, then the steady wail of total heartbreak. I had been praying for this, and did not begrudge the strength it cost her.

By the time she fell off the edge into sleep, she had cried for so long that every muscle in my body ached from sitting still. She never felt me get up, stiff and clumsy as I was. There was something different about her sleeping face now. It was not slack but relaxed. I limped out, feeling as close to peace as I had since I arrived, and as I was passing the living room on the way to the liquor, I heard the phone.

As I had before, I looked over the caller. The picture was undercontrasted and snowy: it was a pay phone. He looked like a construction worker, massive and florid and neckless, almost brutish. And, at the moment, under great stress. He was crushing a hat in his hands, mortally embarrassed. I mentally shrugged and accepted.

"Sharon, don't hang up," he was saying. "I gotta find out what this is all about!"

Nothing could have made me hang up.

"Sharon? Sharon, I know you're there. Jo Ann says you ain't there, she says she called you every day for almost a week and banged on your door a few times. But I know you're there, now anyway. I walked past your place an hour ago and I seen the bathroom light go on and off. Sharon, will you please tell me what the hell is going on? Are you listening to me? I know you're listening to me. Look, you gotta understand, I thought it was all set, see? I mean I thought it was *set*. Arranged. I put it to Jo Ann, cause she's my regular, and she says not me, lover, but I know a gal. Look, was she lying to me or what? She told me for another bill you play them kind of games, sometimes."

Regular two-hundred-dollar bank deposits plus a cardboard box full of scales, vials, razor, mirror, and milk powder makes her a coke dealer—right, Travis McGee? Don't be misled by the fact that the box was shoved in a corner, sealed with tape, and covered with dust. After all, the only other illicit profession that pays regular sums at regular intervals is hooker, and two bills a time is too much for square-jawed, hook-nosed, wide-eyed little Karen, breasts or no breasts.

For a garden-variety hooker . . .

"Dammit, she told me she *called* you and set it up, she give me your *apartment* number." He shook his head violently. "I can't make no sense out of this. Dammit, she *couldn't* be lying

119

to me. It don't figure. You let me in, didn't even turn the camera on first, it was all arranged. Then you screamed and . . . look, I was real careful not to really hurt you, I know I was. Just bruises, Jo Ann said bruises was okay. Then I put on my pants and I'm putting the envelope on the dresser and you bust that chair on me and come at me with that knife and I hadda bust you one. It just don't make no sense, will you *goddammit say something to me?* I'm twisted up inside going on two weeks now. I can't even eat."

I went to shut off the phone, and my hand was shaking so bad I missed, spinning the volume knob to minimum. "Sharon you gotta believe me," he hollered from far far away, "I'm into rape *fantasy,* I'm not into rape!" and then I had found the right switch and he was gone.

I got up very slowly and toddled off to the liquor cabinet, and I stood in front of it taking pulls from different bottles at random until I could no longer see his face—his earnest, baffled, half-ashamed face.

Because his hair was thin sandy blond, and his jaw was a bit too square, and his nose was a trifle hooked, and his blue eyes were just the least little bit too far apart. They say everyone has a double somewhere. And Fate is such a witty little motherfucker, isn't he?

I don't remember how I got to bed.

I woke later that night with the feeling that I would have to bang my head on the floor a couple of times to get my heart started again. I was on my makeshift doss of pillows and blankets beside her bed, and when I finally peeled my eyes open she was sitting up in bed staring at me. She had fixed her hair somehow, and her nails were trimmed. We looked at each other for a long time. Her color was returning somewhat, and the edge was off her bones.

She sighed. "What did Jo Ann say when you told her?"

I said nothing.

"Come on, Jo Ann's got the only other key to this place, and she wouldn't give it to you if you weren't a friend. So what did she say?"

I got painfully up out of the tangle and walked to the window. A phallic church steeple rose above the low-rises a couple of blocks away.

"God is an iron," I said. "Did you know that?"

I turned to look at her and she was staring. She laughed experimentally, stopped when I failed to join in. "And I'm a pair of pants with a hole scorched through the ass?"

"If a person who indulges in gluttony is a glutton, and a person who commits a felony is a felon, then God is an iron. Or else He's the dumbest designer that ever lived."

Of a thousand possible snap reactions, she picked the most flattering and hence most irritating. She kept silent, kept looking at me, and thought about what I had said. At last she said, "I agree. What particular design screwup did you have in mind?"

"The one that nearly left you dead in a pile of your own shit," I said harshly. "Everybody talks about the new menace, wireheading, eighth most common cause of death in less than a decade. Wireheading's not new at all—it's just a technical refinement."

"I don't follow."

"Are you familiar with the old cliché, 'Everything in the world I like is either illegal, immoral, or fattening'?"

"Sure."

"Didn't that ever strike you as damned odd? What's the most nutritionally useless and physiologically dangerous 'food' substance in the world? White sugar. Glucose. And it seems to be beyond the power of the human nervous system to resist it. They put it in virtually all the processed food there is, which is next to all the food there is, because *nobody can resist it*. And so we poison ourselves and whipsaw our dispositions and rot our teeth. Maltose is just as sweet, but it's less popular, precisely because it doesn't kick your blood sugar in the ass and then depress it again. Isn't that odd? There is a primitive programming in our skulls that rewards us, literally overwhelmingly, every time we do something damned silly. Like smoke a poison, or eat or drink or snort or shoot a poison. Or *overeat good* foods. Or engage in complicated sexual behavior without procreative intent, which, if it were not for the pleasure, would be pointless and insane. And which, if pursued for the pleasure alone, quickly becomes pointless and insane anyway. A suicidal brain-reward system is built into us."

"But the reward system is for survival."

"So how the hell did ours get wired up so that survival-threatening behavior gets rewarded best of all? Even the pro-survival pleasure stimuli are wired so that a dangerous *overload* produces the maximum pleasure. On a purely biological level, man is programmed to strive hugely for more than he needs, more than he can profitably use. Add in intelligence and everything goes to hell. Man is capable of outgrowing any ecological niche you put him in—he survives at all because he is The Animal That Moves. Given half a chance he kills himself of surfeit."

My knees were trembling so badly I had to sit down. I felt feverish and somehow larger than myself, and I knew I was talking much too fast. She had nothing whatever to say—with voice, face, or body.

"It is illuminating," I went on, fingering my aching nose, "to note that the two ultimate refinements of hedonism are the pleasure of cruelty and the pleasure of the despoliation of innocence. Consider: no sane person in search of sheerly physical sexual pleasure would select an inexperienced partner. Everyone knows that mature, experienced lovers are more competent, confident, and skilled. Yet there is not a skin mag in the world that prints pictures of men or women over twenty if they can possibly help it. Don't tell me about recapturing lost youth: the root is that a fantasy object over twenty cannot plausibly possess innocence, can no longer be corrupted.

"Man has historically devoted *much* more subtle and ingenious thought to inflicting cruelty than to giving others pleasure—which, given his gregarious nature, would seem a much more survival-oriented behavior. Poll any hundred people at random and you'll find at *least* twenty or thirty who know all there is to know about psychological torture and psychic castration—and maybe two who know how to give a terrific back rub. That business of your father leaving all his money to the church and leaving you 'a hundred dollars, the going rate'—that was *artistry*. I can't imagine a way to make you feel as good as that made you feel rotten. But for him it must have been pure pleasure."

"Maybe the Puritans were right," she said. "Maybe pleasure is the root of all evil. Oh, God! but life is bleak without it."

"One of my most precious possessions," I went on blindly, "is a button, that my friend Slinky John used to hand-paint and sell below cost. He was the only practicing anarchist I ever met. The button reads: 'GO, LEMMINGS, GO!' A lemming surely feels intense pleasure as he gallops to the sea. His self-destruction is programmed by nature, a part of the very same life force that insisted on being conceived and born in the first place. If it feels good, do it." I laughed, and she flinched. "So it seems to me that God is either an iron, or a colossal jackass. I don't know whether to be admiring or contemptuous."

All at once I was out of words, and out of strength. I yanked my gaze away from hers and stared at my knees for a long time. I felt vaguely ashamed, as befits one who has thrown a tantrum in a sickroom.

After a time she said, "You talk good on your feet."

I kept looking at my knees. "I think I used to be an actor once."

"Will you tell me something?"

"If I can."

"What was the pleasure in putting me back together again?"

I flinched.

"Look at me. There. I've got a half-ass idea of what shape I was in when you met me, and I can guess what it's been like since. I don't know if I'd have done as much for Jo Ann, and she's my best friend. You don't look like a guy your favorite kick is sick fems, and you sure as *hell* don't look like you're so rich you got time on your hands. So what's been your pleasure, these last few days?"

"Trying to understand," I snapped. "I'm nosy."

"And do you understand now?"

"Yeah. I put it together."

"So you'll be going now?"

"Not yet," I said automatically. "You're not—"

And caught myself.

"There's something else besides pleasure," she said. "Another system of reward, only I don't think it has much to do with the one I got wired up to my scalp here. Not brain-reward. Call it mind-reward. Call it . . . joy. The thing like pleasure that you feel when you've done a good thing or passed up a real tempting chance to do a bad thing. Or when the unfolding of the universe just seems especially apt. It's nowhere near as flashy and intense as pleasure can be. *Believe* me! But it's got *some*thing going for it. Something that can make you do without pleasure, or even accept a lot of pain, to get it.

"That stuff you're talking about, that's there, that's true. But you said yourself, Man is the animal that outgrows and moves. Evolution works slow, is all." She pushed hair back from her face. "It took a couple of million years to develop a thinking ape, and you want a smart one in a lousy few hundred thou? That lemming drive you're talking about is there—but there's another kind of drive, another kind of force that's working against it. Or else there wouldn't still be any people and there wouldn't be the words to have this conversation and—" She paused, looked down at herself. "And I wouldn't be here to say them."

"That was just random chance."

She snorted. "What isn't?"

"Well, that's *fine*," I shouted. "That's *fine*. Since the world is saved and you've got everything under control I'll just be going along."

I've got a lot of voice when I yell. She ignored it utterly, continued speaking as if nothing had happened. "Now I can say that I have sampled the spectrum of the pleasure system at both ends—none and all there is—and I think the rest of my life I will dedicate myself to the middle of the road and see how that works out. Starting with the very weak tea and toast I'm going to ask you to bring me in another ten minutes or so. With maltose. But as for this other stuff, this joy thing, that I would like to begin learning about, as much as I can. I don't really know a God damned thing about it, but I understand it has something to do with sharing and caring and what did you say your name was?"

"It doesn't matter," I yelled.

"All right. What can *I* do for *you?*"

"Nothing!"

"What did you come here for?"

I was angry enough to be honest. "To burgle your fucking apartment!"

Her eyes opened wide, and then she slumped back against the pillows and laughed until the tears came, and I tried and could not help myself and laughed too, and we shared laughter for a long time, as long as we had shared her tears the night before.

And then, straight-faced, she said, "Wait'll I'm on my feet; you're gonna need help with those stereo speakers. Butter on the toast."

Soul Search

Rebecca Howell stood beside the Plexiglas tank that contained the corpse of her husband Archer, trembling with anticipation. A maelstrom of conflicting emotions raged within her: fondness, yearning, awe, lust, triumphant satisfaction, fierce joy and an underlay of fear all trying to coexist in the same skull. Perhaps no one in all human history had experienced that precise mix of emotions, for her situation was close to unique. Because she was who and what she was, it would shortly lead her to develop the first genuinely new motive for murder in several thousand years.

"Go ahead," she said aloud, and eight people in white crowded around the transparent cryotank with her. In practiced silence, they began doing things.

John Dimsdale touched her shoulder. "Reb," he said softly, "come on. Let them work."

"No."

"Reb, the first part is *not* pretty. I think you should—"

"Dammit, I know that!"

"I think," he repeated insistently, "you should come with me."

She stiffened; and then she saw some of the things the technicians were doing. "All right. Doctor Bharadwaj!"

One of the white-suited figures looked up irritably.

"Call me before you fire the pineal. Without fail." She let Dimsdale lead her from the room, down white tile corridors to Bharadwaj's offices. His secretary looked up as they entered, and hastened to open the door leading into the doctor's inner sanctum for them. Dimsdale dismissed him, and Howell sat down heavily in the luxurious desk chair, putting her feet up on Bharadwaj's desk. They were both silent for several minutes.

"Eight years," she said finally. "Will it really work, John?"

"No reason why it shouldn't," he said. "Every reason why it should."

"It's never been done before."

"On a human, no; not successfully. But the problems have been solved. It worked with those cats, didn't it? And that ape?"

"Yes, but—"

"Look, Bharadwaj knows perfectly well you'll have his skull for an ashtray if he fails. Do you think he'd try it at all if he weren't certain?"

After a pause she relaxed. "You're right, of course." She looked at him then, really seeing him for the first time that day, and her expression softened. "Thank you, John. I . . . thank you for everything. This must be even harder for you than it—"

"Put it out of your mind."

"I just feel so—"

"There is nothing for you to feel guilt over, Reb," he insisted. "I'm fine. When . . . when love cannot possess, it is content to serve."

She started. "Who said that?"

Dimsdale blushed. "Me," he admitted. "About fifteen years ago." *And frequently thereafter,* he added to himself. "So put it out of your mind, all right?"

She smiled. "As long as you know how grateful I am for you. I could never have maintained Archer's empire without you."

"Nonsense. What are your plans—after, I mean?"

"When he's released? As few as possible. I thought perhaps he might enjoy a cruise around the world, sort of a reorientation. But I'm quite content to hole up in Luna or up in Alaska instead—or whatever he wants. As long as I'm with him, I . . ."

He knew precisely how she felt. After this week it might be weeks or years before he saw her again.

The phone rang, and he answered it. "Right. Let's go, Reb. They're ready."

The top of the cryotank had been removed now, allowing direct access to Archer Howell's defrosted body. At present it was only a body—no longer a corpse, not yet a man. It was "alive" in a certain technical sense, in that an array of machinery circulated its blood and pumped its lungs—but it was not yet Archer Howell. Dr. Bharadwaj awaited Rebecca Howell's command, as ordered, before firing the complex and precise charge through the pineal gland that he believed would restore independent life-function—and consciousness—to the preserved flesh.

"The new liver is in place and functioning correctly," he told her when she arrived. "Indications are good. Shall I—"

"At once."

"Disconnect life support," he snapped, and this was done. As soon as the body's integrity had been restored, he pressed a button. The body bucked in its Plexiglas cradle, then sank back limply. A technician shook her head, and Bharadwaj, sweating prodigiously, pressed the button a second time. The body spasmed again—and the eyes opened. The nostrils flared, and drew in breath; the chest expanded; the fingers clenched spasmodically. Rebecca Howell cried out. Dimsdale stared with round eyes, Bharadwaj and his support team broke out in broad grins of relief and triumph . . .

And the first breath was expelled. In a long, high, unmistakably infantile wail.

Rebecca Howell's mind was both tough and resilient. The moment her subconscious decided she was ready to handle consciousness again, it threw off heavy sedation like a flannel blanket. The physician monitoring her telemetry in the next room started violently, wondering if he could have cat-napped without realizing it.

"What's wrong?" Dimsdale demanded.

"Nothing. Uh, she—a second ago she was deep under, and—"

"—now she's wide awake," Dimsdale finished. "All right, stand by." He got up stiffly and went to her door. "Now comes the hard part," he said, too softly for the other to hear. Then he squared his shoulders and went in.

"Reb . . ."

"It's all right, John. Truly—I'm okay. I'm terribly disappointed, of course, but when you look at it in perspective this is just a minor setback."

"No," he said very quietly. "It isn't."

"Of course it is. Look, it's perfectly obvious what's happened. Some kind of cryonic trauma wiped his mind. All his memories are gone, he'll have to start over again as an infant. But *he's got a mature brain,* John. He'll be an adult again in ten years, you wait and see if he isn't. I *know* him. Oh, he'll be different. He won't be the man I knew, he'll have no memories in common with that man, and the new 'upbringing' is bound to alter his personality some. I'll have to learn how to make him love me all over again. But *I've got my Archer back!*"

Dimsdale was struck dumb—as much by admiration for her indomitable spirit as by reluctance to tell her that she was dead wrong. He wished there were some honourable way he could die himself.

"What's ten years?" she chattered on, oblivious. "Hell, what's twenty years? We're both forty, now that I've caught up with him. With the medical *we* can afford, we're both good for a century and a quarter. At least sixty more *years* we can have together, that's four times as long as we've already had. I can be patient another decade or so for that." She smiled, then made herself become businesslike. "I want you to start making arrangements for his care at once. I want him to have the best rehabilitation this planet can provide, the ideal child-hood. *I* don't know what kind of experts we need to hire, you'll have to—"

"No!" he cried.

She started, and looked at him closely. "John, what in God's name is wrong with—" She paled. "Oh my God, they lost him, didn't they?"

"No," he managed to say. "No, Reb, they haven't lost him. They never had him."

"What the fuck are you talking about?" she blazed. "I heard him cry, saw him wave his arms and piss himself. He was *alive*."

"He still is. Was when I came in here, probably still is. But he is not Archer Howell."

"What are you saying?"

"Bharadwaj said a lot I didn't understand. Something about brain waves, something about radically different indices on the something-or-other profile, something about different reflexes and different—he was close to babbling. Archer was born after the development of brain-scan, so they have tapes on him from infancy. Eight experts and two computers agree: Archer Howell's body is alive down the hall, but that's not him in it. Not even the infant Archer. Someone completely different." He shuddered. "A new person. A new, forty-year-old person."

The doctor outside was on his toes, feeding tranquilizers and sedatives into her system in a frantic attempt to keep his telemetry readings within acceptable limits. But her will was a hot sun, burning the fog off her mind as fast as it formed. "Impossible," she cried, and sprang from the bed before Dimsdale could react, ripping loose tubes and wires. "You're wrong, all of you. That's my Archer!"

The doctor came in the door fast, trained and ready for anything; she kicked him in the stomach and leaped over him as he went down. She was out the door and into the hallway before Dimsdale could reach her.

When he reached the room assigned to Archer Howell, Dimsdale found her sitting beside the bed, crooning softly and rocking back and forth. An intern and a nurse were sprawled on the floor, the nurse bleeding slowly from the nose. Dimsdale looked briefly at the diapered man on the bed, and glanced away. He had once liked Archer Howell a great deal. "Reb—"

She glanced up and smiled. The smile sideswiped him.

"He knows me. I'm sure he does. He smiled at me." As she spoke, a flailing hand caught one of hers, quite by accident. "See?" It clutched, babylike, but with adult strength; she winced, but kept the smile.

Dimsdale swallowed. "Reb, it's not him. I swear it's not. Bharadwaj and Nakamura are absolutely—"

The smile was gone now. "Go away, John. Go far away, and don't ever come back. You're fired."

He opened his mouth, and then spun on his heel and left. A few steps down the hall he encountered Bharadwaj, alarmed and awesomely drunk. "She knows?"

"If you value your career, Doctor, leave her be. She knows—and she doesn't believe it."

Three years later she summoned him. Responding instantly cost him a great deal, but he ignored that. He was at her Alaskan retreat within an hour of the summons, slowed only by her odd request that he come alone, in disguise, and without telling anyone. He was conveyed to her den, where he found her alone, seated at her desk. Insofar as it was possible for one of her wealth and power, she looked like hell.

"You've changed, Reb."

"I've changed my mind."

"That surprises me more."

"He's the equivalent of a ten or twelve year old in a forty-three-year-old body. Even allowing for all that, he's not my Archer."

"You believe in brain-scans now?"

"Not just them. I found people who knew him at that age. They helped me duplicate his upbringing as closely as possible." Dimsdale could not guess how much that had cost, even in money. "They agree with the scans. It's not Archer."

He kept silent.

"How do you explain it, John?"

"I don't."

"What do you think of Bharadwaj's idea?"

"Religious bullshit. Or is that redundant? Superstition."

"When you have eliminated the impossible . . ." she began to quote.

"—there's nothing left," he finished.

"If you cannot think of a way to prove or disprove a proposition, does that make it false?"

"*Damn* it, Reb! Do you mean to tell me you're *agreeing*

with that hysterical Hindu? Maybe he can't help his heritage—but *you?*"

"Bharadwaj is right."

"Jesus Christ, Rebecca," he thundered, "is this what love can do to a fine mind?"

She overmatched his volume. *"I'll thank you to respect that mind."*

"Why should I?" he said bitterly.

"Because it's done something no one ever did in all history. I said you cannot think of a way to prove or disprove Bharadwaj's belief. No one ever has." Her eyes flashed. *"I can. I did."*

He gaped at her. Either she had completely lost her mind, or she was telling the truth. They seemed equally impossible.

At last he made his choice. "How?"

"With my desk. Its brain was more than adequate, once mine told it what to do. I'm astonished it never occurred to anyone before."

"You proved the doctrine of reincarnation. With your desk."

"With the computers it has access to. That's right."

He found a chair and sat down. Her hand moved, and the chair's arm emitted a drink. He gulped it gratefully.

"It was so simple, John. I picked an arbitrary date twenty-five years ago, picked an arbitrary hour and minute. That's as close as I could refine it: death records are seldom kept to the second. But it was close enough. I got the desk to—"

"—collect all the people who died or were born at that minute," he cried, slopping his drink. "Of course!"

"I told you. Oh, there were holes all over. Not all deaths are recorded, not by a damn sight, and not all of the recorded ones are nailed down to the minute, even today. The same with birth records, of course. And the worst of it was that picking a date that far back meant that a substantial number of the deaders were born before brain-scan, giving me incomplete data."

"But you *had* to go that far back," he said excitedly, "to get live ones with jelled personalities to compare."

"Right," she said, and smiled approvingly.

"But with all those holes in the data—"

"John, there are fifteen billion people in the solar system. That's one hell of a statistical universe. The desk gave me a tentative answer. Yes. I ran it fifteen more times, for fifteen more dates. I picked one two years ago, trading off the relative ambiguity of immature brain-scans for more complete records. I got fifteen tentative yeses. Then I correlated all fifteen and got a definite yes."

"But—but damn it all to hell, Reb, the fucking *birthrate* has been rising since forever! Where the hell do the *new ones* come from?"

She frowned. "I'm not certain. But I note that the animal birthrate *declines* as the human increases."

His mouth hung open.

"Do you see, John? *You're* a religious fanatic too. The only difference between you and Bharadwaj is, he's right. Reincarnation exists."

He finished his drink in a gulp, milked the chair for more.

"When we froze Archer, he *died*. His soul went away. He was recycled. When we forced life back into his body, his soul was elsewhere engaged. We got pot luck."

The whiskey was hitting him. "Any idea who?"

"I think so. Hard to be certain, of course, but I believe the man we revived was a grade three mechanic named Big Leon. He was killed on Luna by a defective lock-seal, at the right instant."

"Good Christ." He got up and began pacing around the room. "Is that why there are so many freak accidents? Every time you conceive a child you condemn some poor bastard? Of all the grotesque—" He stopped in his tracks, stood utterly motionless for a long moment, and whirled on her.

"Where is Archer now?"

Her face might have been sculpted in ice. "I've narrowed it down to three possibilities. I can't pin it down any better than that. They're all eleven years old, of course. All male, oddly enough. Apparently we don't change sex often. Thank God."

Dimsdale was breathing heavily. "Rebecca," he began dangerously.

She looked him square in the eyes. "I've had a fully equipped cryotheater built into this house. His body's already refrozen. There are five people in my employ who are competent to set this up so it cannot possibly be traced back to me. There is not one of them I can trust to have that much power over me. You are the only person living I trust that much, John. And you are not in my employ, which is another plus."

"God damn it—"

"This is the only room in the system that I am certain is not bugged, John. I want three *perfectly* timed, untraced murders."

"But the bloody cryotechs are *witnesses*—"

"To what? We freeze and thaw him again, hoping it will bring him out of it somehow. From the standpoint of conventional medicine it's as good an idea as any. No one listened to Bharadwaj, there *is* no accepted explanation for Archer's change. And no one but you and I know the real one for certain—even the desk doesn't remember." She snorted. "Nine more attempted defrostings since Archer, none of 'em worked, and *still* nobody's guessed. There's a moratorium on defrosting, but it's unofficial. *We can do it, John.*" She stopped, and sat back in her chair, became totally expressionless. "If you'll help me."

He left the room, left the house, and kept going on foot. Four days later he re-emerged from the forest, bristling with beard, his cheeks gaunt, his clothes torn and filthy. Most of his original disguise was gone, but he was quite unrecognizable as John Dimsdale. The security people who had monitored him from a distance conveyed him to her, as they had been ordered, and reluctantly left him alone with her.

"I'm your man," he said as soon as they had gone.

She winced, and was silent for a long time.

"You'll have to kill Bharadwaj too," she said at last.

"I know."

Rebecca Howell gazed again at the defrosted thing that had once been Archer Howell, but the torrent of emotions was tamed this time, held in rigid control. *It may not work on this shot,* she reminded herself. *I'm only guessing that his soul will have an affinity for his old body. He may end up in a crib in Bombay, this time.* She smiled. *But sooner or later I'll get him.*

"*Señora,* it would be well to do it now."

The smile vanished and she turned to the chief surgeon. "Doctor Ruiz-Sanchez, I said 1200 hours. To the second. You have made me repeat myself."

Her voice was quite gentle, and a normal man would have gone very pale and shut up, but good doctors are not normal men. "*Señora,* the longer he is on machine life-support—"

"HUMOR ME!" she bellowed, and he sprang back three steps and tripped over a power cable, landing heavily on his back. Technicians jumped, then became expressionless and looked away. Ruiz-Sanchez got slowly to his feet, flexing his fingers. He was trembling. "*Si, señora.*"

She turned away from him at once, returned to contemplation of her beloved. There was dead silence in the cryotheater, save for the murmur and chuckle of life-support machinery and the thrum of powerful generators. Cryotechnology was astonishingly power-thirsty, she reflected. The "restarter" device alone drank more energy than her desk, though it delivered only a tiny fraction of that to the pineal gland. She disliked the noisy, smelly generators on principle, but a drain this large *had to* be unmetered. Especially if it had to be repeated several times. *Mass murder is easy,* she thought. *All you need is a good mind and unlimited resources. And one trusted friend.*

She checked the wall-clock. It lacked five minutes of noon. The tile floor felt pleasantly cool to her bare feet; the characteristic cryotheater smell was subliminally invigorating. "Maybe this time, love," she murmured to the half-living body. "Maybe not. But soon."

The door banged open and a guard hurled backward into the room, landing asprawl. Dimsdale stepped over him, breathing hard. He was wild-eyed and seemed drunk.

Only for the barest instant did shock paralyze her, and even for that instant only the tightening of the corners of her mouth betrayed her fury at his imprudence.

"Señor," Ruiz-Sanchez cried in horror, "you are not sterile!"

"No, thank God," Dimsdale said, looking only at her.

"What are you doing here, John?" she asked carefully.

"Don't you see, Reb?" He gestured like a beggar seeking alms. "Don't you see—it's all got to *mean* something. If it *is* true, there's got to be a point to it, some kind of purpose. Maybe we get just a hair smarter each time round the track. A bit more mature. Maybe we *grow.* Maybe what you're trying to do is get him demoted. I've studied all three of them, and so help me God every one of them is making more of his childhood than Archer did. They may not grow up to be as successful as he was. But they'll be happier."

Her voice cracked like a whip now. "John! *This room is not secure.*"

He started, and awareness came into his eyes. He glanced around at terrified doctors and technicians.

"Rebecca, I studied them all first hand. I made it my business. I had to. Three eleven-year-old boys, Rebecca. They have parents. Grandparents. Brothers and sisters, playmates, hopes and dreams. They have *futures,*" he cried, and stopped. He straightened to his full height and met her eyes squarely. "I will not murder them, even for you. I can't."

"*Madre de Dios,* no!" Ruiz-Sanchez moaned in terror. The anesthesiologist began singing his death-song, softly and to himself. A technician bolted hopelessly for the door.

Rebecca Howell screamed with rage, a hideous sound, and slammed her hands down on the nearest console. One hand shattered an irrigator, which began fountaining water. "You *bastard,*" she raged. "You filthy bastard!"

He did not flinch. "I'm sorry. I thought I could."

She took two steps backward, located a throwable object and let fly. It was a tray of surgical instruments.

Dimsdale stood his ground. The tray itself smashed into his mouth, and a needle-probe stuck horribly in his shoulder. Technicians began fleeing.

"Reb," he said, blood starting down his chin, "whoever orders this incredible circus, you and your fucking desk can't outwit Him! Archer *died,* eleven years ago. You cannot have him back. If you'll only *listen* to me, I can—"

She screamed again and leaped for him. Her intention was plainly to kill him with her hands, and he knew she was more than capable of it, and again he stood his ground.

And saw her foot slip in the puddle on the floor, watched one flailing arm snarl in the cables that trailed from the casing of the pineal restarter and yank two of them loose, saw her land face first in water at the same instant as the furiously sparking cables, watched her buck and thrash and begin to die.

Frantically he located the generator that fed the device and sprang for it. Ruiz-Sanchez blocked his way, holding a surgical laser like a dueling knife. Dimsdale froze, and the doctor locked eyes with him. Long after his ears and nose told him it was too late, Dimsdale stood motionless.

At last he slumped. "Quite right," he murmured softly.

Ruiz-Sanchez continued to aim the laser at his heart. They were alone in the room.

"I have no reason to think this room has been bugged by anyone but Rebecca," Dimsdale said wearily. "And the only thing you *know* about me is that I won't kill innocent people. Don't try to understand what has happened here. You and your people can go in peace; I'll clean up. I won't even bother threatening you."

Ruiz-Sanchez nodded and lowered the laser.

"Go collect your team, Doctor, before they get themselves into trouble. You will certify her accidental death for me. Yes?"

The doctor nodded again and began to leave.

"Wait."

He turned. Dimsdale gestured toward the open cryotank. "How do I pull the plug on this?"

Ruiz-Sanchez did not hesitate. "The big switch. There, by the coils at this end." He left.

An hour and a half later, Dimsdale had achieved a meeting of minds with her chief security officer and her personal secretary, and had been left alone in the den. He sat at her desk and let his gaze rest on the terminal keyboard. At this moment thousands of people were scurrying and thinking furiously; her whole mammoth empire was in chaos. Dimsdale sat at its effective center, utterly at peace. He was in no hurry; he had all the time in the world, and everything he had ever wanted.

We do get smarter every time, he thought. *I'm sure of it.*

He made the desk yield up the tape of what had transpired in the cryotheater, checked one detail of the tape very carefully, satisfied himself that it was the only copy, and wiped it. Then, because he was in no hurry, he ordered scotch.

When she's twenty, I'll only be fifty-seven, he thought happily. *Not even middle-aged. It's going to work. This time it's going to work for* both *of us.* He set down the scotch and told the desk to locate him a girl who had been born at one minute and forty-three seconds before noon. After a moment, it displayed data.

"Orphan, by God!" he said aloud. "That's a break."

He took a long drink of scotch on the strength of it, and then he told the desk to begin arranging for the adoption. But it was the courtship he was thinking about.

LOCAL CHAMP

With a depressingly large part of his consciousness, the Warlock watched the damned fool who was trying to kill him this time.

Depressing because it rubbed his nose in the fact that he simply had nothing more pressing to think about. He had not sunk so low that assassins threatened him; rather he had risen so high that they were a welcome relief from boredom.

You must understand that he was unquestionably and indisputably the mightiest Warlock the world had ever known; for twice ten thousand years he had *owned* it. It was barely within the realm of conceivability that another *as* mighty as he *could* simultaneously exist, but they could no more have escaped each other's notice than two brontosaurs in the same pond. There had never been such a one.

Further, he was invulnerable. Not just physically, although that was nice of course, but *really*. A warlock—any sorcerer—can only be truly destroyed by a spell using his name, and it had been thrice five thousand years since the last living being who knew the Warlock's name had gone down to the final death. Since that time he had induced certain subtle mutations in the human race, so that no man now living could have pronounced his name had they known it. His most deadly secret was literally unstealable.

He suffered other minor wizards to live and work, since they kept life interesting and made tolerable servants; when they reached their two thousandth birthday he methodically killed or utterly destroyed them as indicated. He could never be seriously challenged.

In a way he was almost flattered by this latest would-be assassin. Though the Warlock had spent centuries becoming the nastiest and most sadistic being it was within him to be (which was considerable), it had been a long time since anyone had hated him even more than they feared him. When the bugs always scurry away, you lose the fun of stepping on them. He felt something very like fondness for this gallant little bug, amused approval of its audacity. Briefly he contemplated an act of mercy: allowing the poor wretch to live out its two thousand years, in utter agony, and then simply killing it. Anyone who knows anything knows that even two thousand years of torment and physical death are preferable to the real death, the final extinction. The most unpleasant points on the Wheel of Karma are infinitely preferable to the awful emptiness within which it turns.

But even that much charity was alien to the Warlock; the impulse passed. Besides, great wizards (and the occasional especially apt sorcerer) reincarnated with their necromantic potential intact, if not mildly amplified, and there was no assurance that this young upstart would profit from the lesson. Humans seldom did. This tendency toward rebelliousness, piquant though it might be, was not after all something a prudent master of the world should encourage. From his high eyrie, the Warlock observed the pitiful pile of junk being raised up against him with perhaps a quarter of his attention, and sighed.

You may, reading between the lines, have acquired the suspicion that the mighty Warlock was something of a secret coward. Well, what kind of man did you think craves that kind of power badly enough to grasp it bare-handed, to do what must be done to get it? This was the Warlock's bane: millennia of utter security had nearly succeeded in boring the beard off him—and yet facing the problem squarely would have entailed admitting that he was too cowardly to permit any change in his circumstances. For the Warlock, millennia of boredom were preferable to even a significant *possibility* that precious irreplaceable he could be hurled from the Wheel. He preferred not to dwell on this, with any part of his consciousness.

Not that this would-be assassin even remotely alarmed him. The portion of his awareness that had absently divined its magical intent, and now idly watched its secret preparations for battle, felt, as has been said, some amusement something like fondness (but not paternal, warlocks are sterile as witches)—but his overriding emotion was something more than scorn but less than true contempt.

Same old fallacies, he thought. *First they acquire a rudimentary mind shield and they get cocky. As though I needed to read their thoughts to outthink them!* He snorted. *And then they put their money on* physical *energies, three times out of five. They discover that magic, deeply rooted in the Earth, is limited to a sphere of a hundred miles around the planet, while physical energies are not, and they decide that that somehow implies a superiority of some kind. Ephemerals!*

He recalled the last really challenging duel he had ever fought, countless centuries before. He and the other had met on the highest peak on Earth, locked eyes for three and a half years, and then touched the tips of their index fingers together. The site of this meeting would one day be called the Marianas Trench, and the concussion had produced even more damage in the Other Plane.

The Warlock looked upon the massive assemblage of machineries which was supposed to threaten his—well, you couldn't say his *life,* even in jest, could you?—his peace of mind, then; and he sneered. This building full of junk was to be raised up against him? (Could you?)

Nothing but a big beam of coherent light, he complained to himself. *Surely that silly creature can deduce that I'm transparent to the entire electromagnetic spectrum? Hell knows it has clues enough; I meditate above the ionosphere for decades at a time. I've a quarter of a mind to let the impertinent little upstart shoot that thing at me before I kill it, just to see its face.*

About that much of his mind considered the question for a few months. (Meanwhile the bulk of his awareness, as it had for the last eight centuries, devoted itself to a leisurely study of how best to mutate human stock so as to increase the central nervous system's capacity to support agony. Mess with the hypothalamus? Add new senses? Subtle, satisfying stuff.)

By hell, I will, decided that quarter of his mind then. *I'll let the impudent cretin fire its toy at me, and I won't even notice! I'll ignore its attack completely, and it will go mad with rage. In fact, I'll be rather nice to it for about a hundred years, and then I'll arbitrarily destroy it for some trivial offense or other. Delicious!*

The quarter of the Warlock's mind which troubled itself with this matter savored the joy of anticipation for several months, so thoroughly in fact that he actually *did* fail to notice when the upstart wizard's harmless energy-bolt passed through the space occupied by his body. The reflex that caused his physical essence to "sidestep" into the Other Plane was so automatic, so unimportant, that it took a few weeks to come to even a quarter of his attention. He chuckled at that.

He also monitored the wizard's frustrated, impotent rage at least on audio and video (those damned mind shields *were* a nuisance sometimes), and found it good. He invested a fortnight in devising a fiendishly offhand destruction for the fool, instructed himself to remember the affair in a century or so, and forgot the matter.

Those came to be called The Last Hundred Years Of Pain, and they were long.

At last like a child recalling a hoarded sweet the Warlock rummaged in his mental pockets and turned out the matter of the hapless wizard. Memory reported that several other shots had been fired without disturbing his peace. The mortal gave every indication of being sobbing mad. Its aim, for instance, had been going to hell for the last two or three decades; some of its shots had missed him by wide margins. He chuckled, and abandoned his century-old plan for destroying the wight without ever acknowledging its attacks.

The hell, I'll tell it. It's more *fun if it knows I've been playing with it.*

At once he was standing before the wizard in the building of futile engines, clothed in fire. In his left hand was a sword that shimmered and crackled; in his right hand was something that could not be looked upon, even by him.

Oddly, considering its displayed stupidity, the ephemeral did not seem surprised to see him. Its anger was gone, as if it had never been; it met his gaze with something absurdly like serenity.

Machines began to melt around them, and the wizard teleported outdoors, the Warlock of course following without thinking about it. They faced each other about five hundred feet above the top of the highest of many local mountains, and they locked eyes.

"You have come to destroy me," the wizard said quietly.

Of course, the Warlock sent, disdaining speech. *Lasers are harmless to me, of course, but they wouldn't be against one of you, and that makes it an insult.* He frowned. *Had you dared attempt a genuine, necromantic assault, I might have been amused enough to simply kill you hideously.* He gestured with the crackling sword at the building below them, which was also crackling now. *But this incompetence must be culled from the breed.*

"We all do what we can," the wizard said.

Indeed. Well, here you go:

He rummaged in his subconscious's name-file, came up with the wizard's true name, which was Jessica, incorporated that name into the thing in his right hand, and reached out toward the mortal, and "Not here!" she cried and was teleporting upward like a stone hurled by a giant, and *Why the hell not?* the Warlock thought as he pursued the creature effortlessly, intrigued enough to let a good sixty or seventy miles go by before deciding that enough was enough and hurling the thing in his right hand after her and averting his eyes.

She died the real death, then. Her soul was destroyed, instantly and forever, in a detonation so fierce that it was almost physically tangible. The Warlock grunted in satisfaction and was about to return to his eyrie, when he noted that the wizard's physical body continued to exist, an empty hulk still hurtling skyward. It chanced that the Warlock had not had lunch that decade.

Straining a bit to reach it before it passed the limits of the sphere of sorcery, he retrieved the corpse and poised there a moment with the crackling sword ready in his left hand.

And felt the mind shield he had accreted over thrice ten thousand years peeled away like the skin of an orange; felt his true name effortlessly extracted from his memory; felt himself *gripped* as though between some monstrous thumb and forefinger and *plucked* from the sphere of his power, yanked over closer to the sun where the light was better; and in the few helpless boiling-blood seconds before he died both kinds of death, the most powerful Warlock in all the history of the world had time to understand three things: that the laser beams had not been aimed at him, that lasers can carry information great distances, and that this world is only one of billions in a sea of infinity.

Then at last the end of all fear came to him, as it had come a century before to Saint Jessica.

ORPHANS OF EDEN

Well, what would *you* have done?

Begin at the front part, Spider:

It was just after two in the morning. I was right here in my office (as we call the dining room in this family), about to write a science fiction story called "Orphans of Eden" on this loyal senescent Macintosh, when he appeared in the doorway from the kitchen, right next to my Lava Lamp. I don't mean "came through the doorway and stopped"; I mean he *appeared,* in the doorway. He sort of shimmered into existence, like a Star Trek transportee, or the ballplayers disappearing into the corn in *Field of Dreams* in reverse. He was my height and age, but of normal weight. His clothing was crazier than a basketball bat. I never did get the hang of the fashion assumptions behind it. I'd like to say the first thing I noticed about it was the ingenious method of fastening, but actually that was the second thing; first I observed that his clothing pointedly avoided covering either genitals or armpits. I kind of liked that. If you lived in a *nice* world, why would you want to hide your smell? He stood with his hands slightly out from his sides, palms displayed, an expectant look on his extraordinarily beautiful face. He didn't look afraid of me, so I wasn't afraid of him. I hit command-S to save my changes (title and a handful of sentences) and forgot that story completely. Forever, now that I think about it.

"When are you from?" I asked him. "Originally, I mean."

I'm not going too fast for you, am I? If a guy materializes in front of you, and you're sober, he *might* be the genius who just invented the transporter beam . . . but if he's dressed funny, he's a time traveler, right? Gotta be. *Thank God the kitchen door was open* had been my very first thought.

He smiled, the kind of pleased but almost rueful smile you make when a friend comes through a practical joke better than you thought he would. "Very good," he told me.

"It was okay, but that's not a responsive answer."

"I'm sorry," he said. "But I can't say I think a lot of the question itself. Still, if it really matters to you, I was born in the year 2146 . . . though we didn't call it that at the time, naturally. Feel better, now?"

He was right: it hadn't been much of a question. Just the only one I could come up with on the spur of the moment. But I thought it small of him to point it out. I mean, what a spur—what a moment! And the information was mildly interesting, if useless. "You don't go around pulling this on *civilians*, do you?" I asked irritably. "You could give somebody a trauma."

"Good Lord, no," he said. "Why, half the other *science fiction writers* alive now would lose sphincter control if I materialized in their workplace like this."

It was some comfort to think that my work might survive at least another hundred and fifty-five years. Unless, of course, he had run across one of my books in the middle of next week. "That's because they think wonder is just another tool, like sex or violence or a sympathetic protagonist."

"Whereas you know it is a religion, a Grail, the Divine Carrot that is the only thing that makes it possible for human beings to ever *get* anywhere without a stick across their ass, yes, it shows in your work. You understand that only by putting his faith in wonder can a man be a moral being. So you're not afraid of me, or compelled to disbelieve in me, and you probably hadn't even gotten around to trying to figure out a way to exploit me until I just mentioned it: you're too busy wondering."

I thought about it. "Well, I'm sorry to say I've been wasting a good deal of time and energy on trying not to look stupid in retrospect—but yes, most of my attention has been on wonder. Before we get to the question and answer section, though, what's your name?"

"Why?" he asked. "There's only one of me."

"Suppose I want to swear at you."

He gave a smaller version of that faintly annoying smile. "Good point. My name is Daniel."

My wife's ex-husband is named Daniel. Also amazing, also faintly annoying at times. "Would you mind if I went and woke up my wife? She'd be sore if I let her sleep through this." Jeanne enjoys looking at very beautiful men. Obviously. Our teenager, on the other hand, would doubtless find a two-hundred-year-old grownup five times more boring than me—and enough music to wake her (the only thing that will do the trick) would probably also wake the tenants downstairs in the basement suite. "And would you care for some coffee?"

He shuddered slightly—then saw my expression. "Sorry. That was for the coffee, not your wife. Imagine I brought you back to a Cro-Magnon's cave, and he offered you refreshments."

My turn to apologize. "Sorry, I wasn't thinking."

"As to Jeanne . . . please don't misunderstand. I would be honoured to meet her under other circumstances, another time. Your collaborations with her are even better than your solo work." I nodded strong agreement. "But if I correctly

151

decipher her input therein, she is a Soto Zen Buddhist and a sentimentalist."

"What's wrong with that?" I demanded.

"Nothing at all. But I seek advice on a practical matter of morality . . . and *you* understand how omelettes are made."

I frowned. "Do you mind if the Cro-Magnon has a little cup of jaguar blood to help him think?"

"This is your house," he said simply.

Well, actually it isn't—I'm a writer; I rent—but I knew what he meant, and agreed with it. I thought about that while I turned another cup of water into dark Tanzanian magic and spooned in sugar and whipped cream. By the time I tipped the Old Bushmill's into the coffee my Irish was up. "Before we start," I said.

"Yes?" He was watching my preparations with the same gravity I'd like to think I could bring to watching an autopsy.

"You have managed to be sufficiently interesting that I will forgive you this once," I said. "But if you *ever again* drop in without phoning ahead first like that, I'll set the cat on you."

He did not quite look wildly around. "Do you have a cat?"

I winced. Smokey was killed a month ago, by some asshole motorist in a hurry. One of the best masters I ever served. "I'll get one if necessary. And I don't want to hear any guff when you reach my answering machine, either. It's always on. People should be grateful I let 'em leave messages."

"Understood and agreed," he said. "And I apologize. But in my defense: what would you have done if I had left a phone message?"

I nodded. "That's why I forgive you this once." I made one last try at hospitality. "I can offer you charcoal-filtered water."

"Thank you, no."

I pointed to a kitchen chair, and took the one across the table from it for myself. He sat beautifully, like a dancer, or one of Jeanne's Alexander Technique students.

I took a long appreciative sip of my Irish coffee. "I'm listening, Daniel," I said.

"Before we start."

"Yeah?"

"When will you begin to get excited?"

"About a minute after you leave, I hope. By then I can afford to."

He nodded. We both knew I was lying; the cup was trembling. He really was trying to be polite.

Why was he trying so hard to be polite?

"You spoke of wanting my advice on a practical matter of morality," I went on. "Is this an ends-justifying-means kind of deal?"

I had succeeded in impressing him. "You have succeeded in impressing me," he said. "Yes."

I sighed. "You've read *Mindkiller*."

He nodded.

It's one of my scarier books. One or two critics, after having had someone literate summarize it for them, have declared that it says the end justifies the means. Beginning for the first time to be a little scared myself, I said, "And have *you* got the secrets of mindwipe and mindwrite?"

"Oh, no," he said convincingly enough to make me relax again.

"What's holding things up?" I asked. "I expected that stuff to come along well before 2040."

"You vastly underestimate the complexity of modeling the brain."

I nodded philosophically. "It's going around these days. Well, I'm relieved, I guess. I had to force that happy ending.

That happens to me a lot in the serious books."

He nodded again. "But you keep doing it. Splendid."

"Thank you." The better the flattery, the warier I become. Back to business. "Then I am to assume that you have another moral dilemma, as sharp as the one faced by Jacques in *Mindkiller?*"

"It is to me. I want you to tell me if I am a monster . . . or simply a victim of my inability not to ask the next question."

"Or both," I pointed out.

"Or both," he agreed.

I took another long gulp of Irish coffee. I've long since worked out to my own satisfaction the one about a writer's responsibility . . . but I'd always known that book would come back to haunt me one day. "Let me get this straight. You have already done . . . whatever this thing is. Some would call it monstrous. And now you want my opinion on whether or not you were right to do it. Why? Since it's too late."

"I need to know if I dare go public—in my own ficton, my own space/time. If I can't persuade you, I can't persuade anybody."

I always had the sneaking idea I'd make a good judge, if only there weren't so damned many laws. Time to find out if I was right. "First tell me your ends. Then your means. If you can do it that way."

"I can approach it that way," he said, "but the ends imply the means. I can put it in a nutshell. I wanted to do meaningful sociological experiments."

I understood him at once, because he was speaking to the heart of the science fiction story I'd intended to write. But in case I only *thought* I understood him, I dragged the exposition out of him like a good character should. "What do you mean?"

"I think you suspect," he said. "Most of the really important questions about human societies are unanswerable because you can't contain the size of the question. You can't understand the ancient Romans if you don't know about all their neighbours and trading partners and subject peoples, and you can't really grasp any of *them* any better because they all influence each other helter skelter—and you can't even get a start on any one of them until you know *their* whole history back to their year one. It's the history that's even worse than the local complexity: so much of any society is vestigial, the original reasons for its fundamental assumptions forgotten.

"And it's the *history* that always gets in the way of trying to make things better. Look at your own contemporary ficton. Can you imagine any solution to the Irish problem or the Serbo-Croatian problem or the Palestinian-Jewish problem or any one of a hundred others like them that does not involve giving everyone involved mass amnesia and erasing all the history books?"

"Well, yes," I said. "But it won't come soon. Now that you tell me telepathy isn't even going to be as easy as time travel."

"For all I know telepathy could come along before 2300," he said. "I left in 2292," (I calculated without much surprise that he was at least a hundred and forty-four subjective years old) "and one of the limitations of time travel—a blessed one in my opinion—is that you cannot go further *forward* in time than you have already been. The only way to see the future is to live it. But I'm not expecting telepathy soon—then/soon—either."

I finished my coffee. "I'm sorry to hear that. Still, there's no real hurry. Once we have telepathy *and* time travel, we can build heaven or a reasonable facsimile retroactively."

"As in your book *Time Pressure*," he agreed. "But since I don't expect that soon and can't depend on it ever, I'm trying to save the human race in a different way. There is some urgency about the matter. When I come from, we have come very close to destroying ourselves in catastrophic warfare."

"Nanotechnological?"

"Worse. I strongly advise you to leave it at that."

I could not suppress the shudder . . . or the squirm that followed it. I had been wondering if he was too evolved to have immunities for primitive local germs—just wondering, not worrying, as I believe a man's health is his business. Now I was reminded that there are circumstances under which a man's health is your business. Was Daniel carrying anything?

Too late to worry now. "What kind of a ficton is it?"

He hesitated. "It's hard to give you a meaningful answer. Imagine I'm a Cro-Magnon. Tell me: what's your world like?"

"Giddy, with fear and pride and guilt and shame, but trying to be as decent as it can."

He nodded thoughtfully. "Okay. In those terms, the 2290s are sullen, scared and preoccupied with the present. In the immediate past is horror, and just beyond that are the things that inexorably brought it on us, and still we prefer not to think overmuch of the future. We see what went wrong, and don't know how to fix it. As near as we can see, all the future holds is another slow painful climb to the pinnacle which blasts all who stand on it, and those of us who think about that wonder what's the point. So not many of us think about it."

I was more grateful than ever to have lived my life in the twentieth century. But I was also puzzled. "It's hard to square that with your clothes. That kind of outfit in that kind of world doesn't ring true. People like that would cover up."

He smiled sadly. "These clothes were designed elsewhen."

Skip irrelevancies. The night was old. "Okay. So what do

you figure to do about your situation?"

He clasped his fingers together before him on the table. With his spine so straight, it made him look as if he were praying. "It's all the history, you see. The weight of all that history, all those mistakes we can't ever undo or forget."

"I can understand that."

"Probably you can; the problem is just now beginning to become apparent. Time was when the maximum length of history was the number of stories an old man could tell before he died. Then we got too damned good at recording and preserving the stories. At about the same time there began to be too many stories, and they all interacted. And then came the Information Explosion. Human beings are only built to tolerate the knowledge of so much failure and tragedy. All the things we've ever done to warp the human spirit, from making wars to making gods, are there in us, at the root of anything we plant, at the base of anything we build. When you try to start all over again from scratch, you find out you can't. Your definition of 'scratch' merely defines the direction history has warped you in, and condemns you to tug in the other direction. But the weave is too complex to straighten.

"It's too late for us to start over. It's too late to try and create a society without taboos: the people who would try it are warped by the knowledge of what a taboo is. It's too late to try and create a society without sexual repression: the parents inevitably pass along to their children at least warped shadows of the repressions they inherited themselves. It's too late to make a society without racism . . . and so on. Every attempt at an experimental Utopian community has failed, no matter how hard they tried to keep themselves isolated from the surrounding world. Sealing yourself up in a self-sustaining space colony and smashing all your comm gear doesn't help. It's just too late to experiment with a society that has no possessions, or conformity, or tribalism, or irrational religions—all possible experimental subjects are compromised by their knowledge of human history. What's needed is some way to put an 'Undo' key on history."

"I think I see where you're going," I said. "I was just about to write a story about—"

"I know," he interrupted. "And you were going to screw it up."

We'll never know, will we? "Go on."

"Well, I think you know the only possible solution. Let's do a thought experiment—I *know* you won't mind the pun. Hypothetically: put a bunch of preverbal children—infants, for preference—in a congenial artificial environment. Plenty of room, plenty of food for the taking, mild climate, no predators, an adequate supply of useful materials and appropriate technology for later. Immunize them against all disease, and give them doctor-robots that will see them into adulthood and then fall apart. Provide AI packages to teach language skills and basic hygiene—both carefully vetted to be as semantically value-free as possible—"

"Have the AI design the language," I suggested.

"Yes. Open-ended, but with just enough given vocabulary to sustain a complicated thought: let 'em invent their own. A clean foundation. When they're ready to handle it, have the machines teach them the basic principles of mathematics and science, using numbers rather than words wherever possible, and just enough philosophy to keep them from brewing up organized religion. And *not a damned word of history.* Then you go away, and come back in a thousand years."

"To find them knifing each other over which one has the right to sacrifice a peasant to the teaching machines," I said.

"You are not really that cynical."

"Of course I am. Why do you think I have to keep writing those happy endings? You know, another writer wrote a story years ago with the same basic theme as your thought experiment—"

"Yes," he said, "and what was the first thing his protagonist did? Saddled the poor little bastards with the author's own religion! Gifted them with shame and sin and an angry but bribeable paternalistic God and a lot of other 'moral' mumbo jumbo. Phooey. He had greatness in his hands and he blew it. That time."

I didn't quite agree, but the differences were quibbles. And I had something else to think about. This wasn't a science fiction story Daniel was describing, or any cockamamie "thought experiment" . . .

I once heard a black woman use some memorable language: she described someone as having been "as ugly as Death backin' out of a outhouse, readin' *Mad* magazine; ugly enough to make a freight train take a dirt road."

All at once a thought uglier than that was slithering around under my hair.

"Talk about cynical," I went on, "why don't we get down to the crucial problem with this little thought experiment, as you call it?"

I was looking him in the eye, and he did not look away. But he didn't answer me either. So I did.

"The problem is, where do you get the infants?"

"Yes," he said slowly, "that was the problem."

I poured more Irish coffee, omitting coffee, cream and sugar. When it was gone I said, "So you're the guy that laid the bad rap on all those gypsies." I was trying hard not to hate him. I try not to hate anybody, no matter how much it seems indicated, until I've walked around it a little while. And he hadn't said he was through talking yet. But so far I really hated this. . . .

He looked confused for the first time since I'd met him; then he got the reference. "No, no. That wasn't me, any more than it was gypsies. As far as I know, that child-stealing gossip was sheer wishful thinking on the part of parents, combined with a natural hatred of anyone who didn't have to stay in the village they were born in. I've never stolen a baby, anywhere in Time."

"Then where did you get them? Roll your own? In a test-tube or a Petri dish or whatever? Were the donors informed volunteers?" Even if the answer was yes, I didn't like this one any better. Call up human beings out of nothingness, to be born (or decanted or whatever) and suffer and die, for purely scientific reasons? At least the first generation of them compelled to grow up without parents or role models, forced to reinvent love and law and humour and a trillion other things I took for granted? If they could? Grow babies as guinea pigs?

"I've never made a baby either," he said. "Not even with someone else's genes."

I frowned. "Den ah give up, Mr. Bones—how *did* dat time-traveler . . . oh." Then I said: "Oh!" And finally: "*Oh!*"

"A lot of infants have been abandoned on a lot of windy hillsides or left in dumpsters since time began," he said sadly. "If Pharaoh's daughter had happened to miss Moses, she probably could have picked up another one the next day. It tends to happen most in places and times where, even if the child had somehow miraculously been found and taken in by some contemporary, it would have had a maximum life expectancy of about thirty years. So I denied some of them the comfort of a nice quick death by exposure or predator, brought them to a safe place and gave them the means to live in good health for hundreds of years."

"And used them as guinea pigs," I said, but without any real heat in it. I was beginning to see his logic.

He didn't duck it. "That's right. Now you tell me: are my actions forgivable?"

"Give me a minute," I said, and poured more whiskey and thought.

Thou shalt not use human beings as guinea pigs.

Don't be silly, Spider. Accept that and you've just tossed out most of medicine. Certainly all the vaccines. *First* you use guinea pigs, sure . . . but sooner or later you have to try it on a human or you're just a veterinarian. And meanwhile people are *dying,* in pain . . .

Thou shalt not experiment on human beings without their informed consent.

Many valuable psych experiments collapse with informed consent. You can't experiment with the brain chemistry of a schizophrenic without endangering his life. You can't find out whether slapping an hysteric will calm him down by asking him: you have to try it and see what happens. Daniel's too is an experiment which by definition may not have informed consent: informing the subject destroys the experiment. Is there, written anywhere, some fundamental law forbidding a man to withhold information, even if he believes it to be potentially harmful?

Thou shalt not use infants as guinea pigs.

Hogwash, for the same reasons as number one above. How do you test an infant-mortality preventative, if not on an infant? Should we not have learned how to do fetal heart surgery? Do not the benefits of amniocentesis outweigh the (please God) few who will inevitably be accidentally skewered? Would Daniel's orphans really be better off dead than in Eden?

Thou shalt not play God.

161

God knows someone has to. Especially if the future is as grim as Daniel says. And She hasn't been answering Her phone lately. When it comes down to the crunch, humans have *always* tried to play God, if they thought they could pull it off . . .

Ah, there was the crux.

"And what kind of results have you gotten?" I asked.

His face split in a broad grin. "Ah, there's the crux, isn't it? If you examine the data that came out of the Nazi death camps, and profit from that terrible knowledge . . . are you any better than Dr. Mengele?"

I winced.

"That is the question I want you to answer," he said. "You are completely insulated from any possible backlash to your answer—the people who will ultimately judge me will never know you were consulted, even after the fact. There is no stick to be applied to you as a result of your answer. And now I will offer the carrot. The same carrot that got me into this."

I was already reaching for the whiskey. *Dammit,* I thought, *this isn't fair. All I ever tried to do was entertain people . . . Balls,* came the answer from deep inside.

"If you tell me that constructing the experiment was a moral act," he went on inexorably, "I will tell you everything I can about the results."

Well, what would you have done?

Not Fade Away

I became aware of him five parsecs away.

He rode a nickel-iron asteroid of a hundred metric tons as if it were an unruly steed, and he broke off chunks of it and hurled them at the stars, and he howled.

I manifested at the outer periphery of his system and waited to be noticed. I'm sure he had been aware of me long before I detected him, but he affected not to see me for several weeks, until my light reached him.

I studied him while I waited. There was something distinctly odd about his morphology. After a while I recognized it: he was wearing the original prototype—the body our ancestors wore! I looked closer, and realized that it was the only body he had ever worn.

Oh, it had been Balanced and spaceproofed and the skull shielded, of course. But he looked as if when Balancing was discovered, he had been just barely young enough for the process to take. He must have been one of the oldest of the Eldest.

But why keep that ridiculous body configuration? It was hopelessly inefficient, suited only to existence on the surface of planets, and rather poorly to that. For a normal environment, everything about it was wrong. I saw that he had had the original sensory equipment improved for space conditions, but it was still limited and poorly placed. Everything about the body was laid out bilaterally and unidirectionally, creating a blind side. The engineering was all wrong, the four limbs all severely limited in mobility. Many of the joints were essentially one-directional, simple hinges.

Stranger still, the body was grotesquely, comically overmuscled. Whenever his back happened to be turned to his star, the forty-kilo bits of rock he hurled achieved system escape velocity—yet he was able to keep that asteroid clamped between his great thighs. What individual ever— much less routinely—needs that much strength in free space?

Oddest of all, of course, his mind was sealed.

Apparently totally. I could get no reading at all from him, and I am a very good reader. He must have been completely unplugged from the Bonding, and in all my three thousand years I have met only four such. He must have been as lonely as any of our ancestors ever was. Yet he knew that the Bonding exists, and refused it.

A number of objects were tethered or strapped to his body, all worn but showing signs of superb maintenance. It took me several days to identify them all positively as utensils, several more to realize that each was a weapon. It takes time for things to percolate down out of the Race Memory, and the oldest things take the most time.

By then he was ready to notice me. He focused one of his howls and directed it to me. He carefully ignored all the part of me that is Bonded, addressing only my individual ego, with great force.

"GO AWAY!"

"Why?" I asked reasonably.

"GO AWAY AT ONCE OR I WILL END YOU!"

I radiated startled interest. "Really? Why would you do that?"

"OH, GAAAH . . ."

There was a silence of some hours.

"I will go away," I said at last, "if you will tell me why you want me to do so."

His volume was lower. "Do you know who I am?"

I laughed. "How could I know? Your mind is sealed."

"I am the last warrior."

"Warrior? Wait now . . . 'warrior.' Must be an old word. 'Warrior.' Oh—*oh*. You kill and destroy. Deliberately. How odd. Are you going to destroy me?"

"I may," he said darkly.

"I see. How might I dissuade you? I do not believe I am old enough to die competently yet, and I have at least one major obligation outstanding."

"Do you lack the courage to flee? Or the wit?"

"I shall attempt to flee if I find it necessary. But I would not expect to succeed."

"Ah. You fear me."

" 'Fear'? No. I recognize the menace you represent. I repeat: how might I dissuade you from ending me? Is there something I can offer you? Access to the Bonding of Minds, perhaps?"

His reply was instant. "If I suspect you of *planning* to initiate the Bonding process with me, I will make your death a thing of unending and unspeakable agony."

I projected startlement, then masked it. "What *can* I do for you, then?"

He laughed. "That's easy. Find me a fair fight. Find me an enemy. If he or she or it is as strong as me, I will let you go unharmed. If stronger, I will give you all I own, and consecrate my death to you."

"I am not sure I understand."

"I am the *last* warrior."

"Yes?"

"When I chose my profession, warriors were common, and commonly admired. We killed or destroyed not for personal gain, but to protect a group of non-warriors, or to protect an idea or an ideal."

I emanated confusion. "Against what?"

His answer was days in coming. "Other warriors."

"How did the cycle get started?"

"Primitive men were all warriors."

"Really?"

"Then there came a time when the average man had to be forced to kill or destroy. One day, he could no longer be forced. A Balanced human in free space cannot be coerced—only slain. Can you visualize circumstances which would force you to kill?"

"Only with the greatest difficulty," I said. "But you enjoy it? You would find pleasure or value in killing me?"

A week passed. At last he smote his asteroid with his fist, sharply enough to cause rock to fly from its other side. "No. I lied. I will not kill you. What good is a fight you can't lose?"

"Why did you . . . 'lie'?"

"In order to frighten you."

"You failed."

"Yes, I know."

"Why did you wish to frighten me?"

"To compel you to my will."

"Hmmm. I believe I see. Then you do wish to locate an enemy. I am baffled. I should have thought a warrior's prime goal to be the elimination of all other warriors."

"No. A warrior's prime goal is to overcome other warriors. I am the greatest warrior our race has ever raised up. I have not worked in over five thousand years. There is no one to overcome."

"Oh."

"Do you know what the R-brain is?"

"Wait. It's coming. Oh. I know what the R-brain *was*. The primitive reptile brain from which the human brain evolved."

"And do you know that for a considerable time, early humans—true humans—possessed, beneath their sentient brains, a vestigial but powerful R-complex, called 'the subconscious mind'?"

"Of course. The First Great Antinomy."

"I have an R-complex."

I registered shock. "You cannot possibly be old enough."

I could sense his bitter grin before the sight of it crawled to me at lightspeed. "Do you notice anything interesting about this particular star-system?"

I glanced around. "Barring your presence in it, no."

"Consider that planet there. The third."

At first glance it was an utterly ordinary planet, like a myriad of others in this out-of-the-way sector. It was wet and therefore alive, and even showed signs that it had evolved intelligent life at least once, but of course that was—by definition—long gone. None of its remaining lifeforms seemed anywhere near bright enough to leave it behind and enter the world yet. Its physical and ballistic properties appeared unremarkable.

But after only a few days of contemplation, I cried out in surprise. "Why . . . its period of rotation is almost *precisely* one standard day. And its period of revolution seems to approximate a standard year. And its surface acceleration is a standard gee. Do you mean to tell me that planet is . . . uh . . . is—"

"Dirt," he agreed. "And yonder star is Sol."

"And you imply that—"

"Yes. I was born here. On that planet, in fact. At a time when all the humans in the universe lived within the confines of this system—and used less than half the planets, at that."

"!!!"

"Do you still wonder that I shun your Bonding?"

"No. To you, with a reptile brain-stem, it must be the ulti-mate obscenity."

"Defenselessness. Yes."

"A thing which can be neither dominated nor compelled. And which itself will not dominate or compel . . . you must hate us."

"Aye."

"You could be healed. The reptile part of your brain could—"

"I could be gelded too. And why not, since none will breed with me? Yet I choose to retain my gonads. And my R-complex. Call it habit."

"I see." I paused in thought. "What prevents you from physically attacking the Bond? I believe that at this point in history, you could harm it greatly . . . perhaps even destroy it."

"I repeat: what good is a fight you can't lose?"

"Oh."

"In the old days . . . there was glory. There was a galaxy to be tamed, empires to be carved out of the sky, mighty ene-mies to challenge. More than once I pulverized a star. With four allies I battled the Ten of Algol, and after two centuries broke them. Then were other sentient races found, in the inner neighboring arm of the galaxy, and I learned the ways of fighting them." He paused. "I was honoured in those days. I was one of mankind's saviors." A terrible chuckle. "Do you know anything sorrier than an unemployed savior?"

"And your fellows?"

"One day it was all changed. The brain had evolved. Man's enemies were broken or co-opted. It became clear that competition for unlimited wealth is insane. Peace broke out. The cursed Bonding began. At first we fought it as a plague swallowing our charges. But ere long we came to see that it was what they had freely chosen. Finally there came a day when we had only ourselves to fight."

"And?"

"We fought. Whole systems were laid waste, alliances were made and betrayed, truly frightening energies were released. The rest of mankind withdrew from us and forgot us."

"I can see how this would be."

"Man had no need of us. Man was in harmony with himself, and his neighbours, and it was now plain that in all the galaxy there were no threatening races extant or imminent. For a long time we had hope that there might be enemies beyond this galaxy—that we might yet be needed. And so we fought mock-combats, preserving ourselves for our race. We dreamed of once again battling to save our species from harm; we dreamed of vindication."

A long pause.

"Then we heard of contact with Bondings of sentient beings from neighboring galaxies. The Unification began. In rage and despair we fell upon each other, and there was a mighty slaughter. There was one last false alarm of hope when the Malign Bonding of the Crab Nebula was found." His voice began to tremble with rage. "We waited for your summons. And you . . . you . . ." Suddenly he screamed. "YOU *CURED* THE BASTARDS!"

"Listen to me," I said. "A neuron is a wonderful thing. But when a billion neurons agree to work together, they become a thing a billion times more wonderful—a brain. A mind. There are as many stars in this galaxy as there are neurons in a single human mind. More than coincidence. This galaxy has *become* a single mind: the Bonding. There are as many galaxies in this universe as there are stars in the average galaxy. Each has, or is developing, its own Bonding. Each of these is to be a neuron in the Cosmic Mind. One day Unification will be complete, and the universe will be intelligent. You can be part of that mind, and share in it."

"*No,*" he said emphatically. "If I am part of the Cosmic Mind, then I am part of its primitive subconscious mind. The subconscious is useful only for preservation from outside threat. As your brain evolved beyond your ancestors' subconscious mind, your universal mind has evolved beyond me. There is nothing in the plenum that you need fear." He leaned forward in sudden pain, embraced his asteroid with his arms as well as his legs. I began moving closer to him, not so rapidly as to alarm him if he should look up, but not slowly.

"When we understood this," he said, "we warriors fell upon each other anew. Four centuries ago Jarl and I allied to defeat The One In Red. That left only each other. We made it last as long as we could. Perhaps it was the greatest battle ever fought. Jarl was very, very good. That was why I saved him for last."

"And you overcame him?"

"Since then I have been alone." He lifted his head quickly and roared at the universe, "Jarl, you son of a bitch, *why didn't you kill me?*" He put his face again to the rock.

I could not tell if he had seen me approaching.

"And in all the years since, you have had no opponent?"

"I tried cloning myself once. Useless. No clone can have my experience and training; the environment which produced me no longer exists. What good is a fight you cannot lose?"

I was coming ever closer. "Why do you not suicide?"

"What good is a fight you cannot lose?"

170

I was near now. "Then all these years, you have prayed for an enemy?"

"Aye." His voice was despairing.

"Your prayer is answered."

He stiffened. His head came up and he saw me.

"I represent the Bonding of the Crab," I said then. "The cure was imperfect," and I did direct at him a laser.

I was near, but he was quick, and his mirror-shield deflected my bolt even before he could have had time to absorb my words. I followed the laser with other energies, and he dodged, deflected or neutralized them as fast as they could be mounted.

There was an instant's pause then, and I saw a grin begin slowly and spread across his face. Carnivore's warning. He flung his own weapons into space.

"I am delivered," he cried, and then he shifted his mass, throwing his planetoid into a spin. When it lay between us, I thought he had struck it with both feet, for suddenly it was rushing toward me. Of course I avoided it easily—but as it passed, he darted around from behind it, where he had been hidden, and grappled with me physically. He had hurled the rock not with his feet, but with a reaction drive.

Then did I understand why he kept such an ancient body-form, for it was admirably suited to single combat. I had more limbs, but weaker, and one by one my own weapons were torn from me and hurled into the void. Meanwhile mental energies surged against each other from both sides, and space began to writhe around us.

Mentally I was stronger than he, for he had been long alone, and mental muscles can be exercised only on another mind. But his physical power was awesome, and his ferocity a thing incomprehensible to me.

And now I see the end coming. Soon his terrible hands will

reach my brain-case and rip it asunder. When this occurs, my body will explode with great force, and we shall both die. He knows this, and in this instant of time before the end, I know what he is doing, beneath his shield where I cannot probe. He is composing his last message for transmission to you, his people, his Bonding. He is warning you of mortal danger. He is telling you where to find his hidden DNA samples, where to find the records he has made of everything he knows about combat, how to train his clones to be *almost* as good as he is. And he is feeling the satisfaction of vindication. *I could have told you!* he is saying. *Ye who knew not my worth, who had forgotten me, yet will I save you!*

This is my own last message to you, to the same people, to the same Bonding. It worked. He believes me. I have accomplished what you asked of me. He has the hero's death he craved.

We will die together, he and I. And that is meet and proper, for I am the last Healer in the cosmos, and now I too am unemployed.

In the Olden Days

George Maugham returned home from work much later than usual, and in a sour frame of mind. He was tired and knew that he had missed an excellent home-cooked meal, and things had not gone well at work despite his extra hours of labour. His face, as he came through the door, held that expression that would cause his wife to become especially understanding.

"Light on in the kids' window," he said crankily as he hung his coat by the door and removed his boots. "It's late."

Luanna Maugham truly was an extraordinary woman. With only a minimal use of her face and the suggestion of a shrug and the single word "Grandpa," she managed to convey amusement and irony and compassion and tolerant acceptance, and thereby begin diffusing his potential grumpiness. He felt the last of it bleed from him as she put into his hands a cup of dark sweetness which he knew perfectly well would turn out to be precisely drinking temperature. He understood how much she did for him.

But he still felt that he should follow up the issue of their children's bedtime. "I wish he wouldn't keep them up so late," he said, pitching his voice to signal his altered motivation.

"Well," she said, "they can sleep in tomorrow morning—

no school. And he does tell fairy tales *so* well, dear."

"It's not the fairy tales I mind," he said, faintly surprised to feel a little of his irritation returning. "I just hope he's not filling their heads with all that other garbage." He sipped from his cup, which was indeed the right temperature. "All those hairy old stories of his. About the Good Old Days When Men Were Men and Women Knew Their Place." He shook his head. Yes, he was losing his good humour again.

"Why do his stories bother you so?" she asked gently. "Honestly, they seem pretty harmless to me."

"I think all that old stuff depresses them. Nightmares and that sort of thing. Confuses them. Boring, too, the same old stuff over and over again."

Mrs. Maugham did *not* point out that their two children never had nightmares, or permitted themselves to be bored. She made, in fact, no response at all, and after a sufficient pause, he shook his head and continued speaking, more hesitantly. "I mean . . . there's something about it I can't . . ." He glanced down at his cup, and perhaps he found there the words he wanted. He sipped them. "Here it is: if the Good Old Days were so good, then I and my generation were fools for allowing things to change—then the world that *we* made is inferior—and I don't think it is. I mean, every generation of kids grows up convinced that their parents are idiots who've buggered everything up, don't they, and I certainly don't want or need *my* father encouraging the kids to feel that way." He wiped his lip with the heel of his hand. "I've worked hard, all my life, to make this a better world than the one I was born into, and . . . and it is, Lu, it *is*."

She took his face in her hands, kissed him, and bathed him in her very best smile. "Of course it is," she lied.

"And that," Grandpa was saying just then, with the warm

glow of the storyteller who knows he has wowed 'em again, "is the story of how Princess Julie rescued the young blacksmith Jason from the Dark Tower, and together they slew the King of the Dolts." He bowed his head and began rolling his final cigarette of the night.

The applause was, considering the size of the house, gratifying. "That was really neat, Grandpa," Julie said enthusiastically, and little Jason clapped his hands and echoed, "Really neat!"

"Now, tomorrow night," he said, and paused to lick his cigarette paper, "I'll tell you what happened *next.*"

"Oh God, yes," Julie said, smacking her forehead, "the Slime Monster, I forgot, he's still loose."

"The Slime Monster!" Jason cried. "But that's my favourite *part!* Grampa tell *now.*"

"Oh yes, please, Grampa," Julie seconded. In point of fact, she was not really all that crazy about the Slime Monster—he was pretty yucky—but now he represented that most precious commodity any child can know: a few minutes more of afterbedtime awakeness.

But the old man had been braced for this. "Not a chance, munchkins. Way past your bedtimes, and your folks'll—"

A chorus of protests rained about his head.

"Can it," he said, in the tone that meant he was serious, and the storm chopped off short. He was mildly pleased by this small reflection of his authority, and he blinked, and when his eyes opened Julie was holding out the candle to light his cigarette for him, and little Jason was inexpertly but enthusiastically trying to massage the right knee which, he knew (and occasionally remembered), gave Grandpa trouble a lot, because of something that Jason understood was called "our fright us." How, the old man wondered mildly, do they manage an instant one-eighty without even shifting gears?

"You can tell us tomorrow, Grampa," Julie assured him, with the massive nonchalance that only a six-year-old girl can lift, "I don't matter about it." She put down the candle and got him an ashtray.

"Yeah," Jason picked up his cue. "Who cares about a dumb old Slime Monster?" He then attempted to look as if that last sentence were sincere, and failed; Julie gave him a dirty look for overplaying his hand.

Little con artists, Grandpa thought fondly, there's hope for the race yet. He waited for the pitch, enjoying the knee-massage.

"I'll make you a deal, Grampa," Julie said.

"A deal?"

"If I can ask you a question you can't answer, you have to tell about the Olden Days for ten minutes."

He appeared to think about it while he smoked. "Seven minutes." There was no timepiece in the room.

"Nine," Julie said at once.

"Eight."

"Eight and a half."

"Done."

The old man did not expect to lose. He was expecting some kind of trick question, but he felt that he had heard most, perhaps all, of the classic conundrums over the course of his years, and he figured he could cobble up a trick answer to whatever Julie had up her sleeve. And she sideswiped him.

"You know that poem, 'Roses are red, violets are blue'?" she asked.

"Which one? There are hundreds."

"That's what I mean," she said, springing the trap. "I know a millyum of 'em. Roses are red, violets are blue—"

"—outhouse is smelly and so are you," Jason interrupted loudly, and broke up.

She glared at her younger brother and pursed her lips. "Don't be such a child," she said gravely, and nearly caught Grandpa smiling. "So that's my question."

"What?"

"Why do they always say that?"

"You mean, 'Roses are red, violets—?'"

"When they're *not*."

"Not what?"

She looked up at the ceiling as though inviting God to bear witness to the impossibility of communicating with grownups. *"Blue,"* she said.

The old man's jaw dropped.

"Violets are *violet*," she amplified.

He was thunderstruck. She was absolutely right, and all at once he could not imagine why the question had not occurred to him decades earlier. "I'll be damned. You win, Princess. I have no idea how that one got started. You've got me dead to rights."

"Oh boy," Jason crowed, releasing Grandpa's knee at once and returning to his bed. "You kids nowadays," he prompted as Julie crawled in beside him.

Grandpa accepted the inevitable.

"You kids nowadays don't know nothin' about nothin'," he said. "Now in the Olden Days . . ."

Grinning triumphantly, Julie fluffed up her pillow and stretched out on the pallet, pulling her blanket delicately up over her small legs, just to the knees. Jason pulled his own blanket to his chin, uncaring that this bared his feet, and stared at the ceiling.

". . . in the Olden Days it wasn't like it is these days. Men were men in them days, and women knew their place in the world. This world has been going straight to hell since I was a boy, children, and you can dip me if it looks like getting any better. Things you kids take for granted nowadays, why, in the Olden Days we'd have laughed at the thought. Sometimes we did.

"F'rinstance, this business of gettin' up at six in the goddam morning and havin' a goddam potato pancake for breakfast, an' then walkin' twenty goddam kilometers to the goddam little red schoolhouse—in the Olden Days there wasn't *none* of that crap. We got up at eight like civilized children, and walked twenty goddam meters to where a *bus* come and hauled us the whole five klicks to a school the likes of which a child like you'll never see, more's the pity."

"Tell about the bus," Jason ordered.

"It was big enough for sixty kids to play in, and it was warm in the winter, sometimes *too* warm, and God Himself drove it, and it smelled wonderful and just the same every day. And when it took you home after school, there was none of this nonsense of grabbing some refried beans and goin' off to haul rock and brush for the goddam road crew for fifty cents a week, I'll tell you that. Why, if a feller had tried to hire me when I was your age, at a good salary, mind you, they'd have locked him up for *exploitin'* me! No sir, we'd come home after a hard day of learning, and we'd play ball or watch TV or read a book, whatever we felt like—ah Christ, we lived like kings and we never even knew it!

"You, Julie, you'll have children before you're sixteen, and a good wife and mother you'll be—but in the Olden Days you might have been an executive, or a doctor, or a dancer. Jason, you'll grow up to be a good farmer—if they don't hang you—but if you'd been born when I was, you could have made movies in Thailand, or flown airliners to Paris, or picked rocks off the goddam face of the Moon and brought 'em home. And before any of that, you both could have had something you're never going to know—a mysterious, terrible, wonderful thing called adolescence.

"But my generation, and your father and mother's, we threw it all away, because it wasn't perfect. The best I can explain it is that they all voted themselves a free lunch, democratic as hell, and then tried to duck out when the cheque arrived. They spent every dime they had, and all of your money besides, and they *still* had to wash some dishes. There was two packs of idiots, you see. On one side you had rich sons of bitches, excuse my language, and they were arrogant. Couldn't be bothered to build a nuclear power plant to specs or a car that worked, couldn't be bothered to hide their contempt. Why, do you know that banks actually used to set out, for the use of their customers, pens that didn't work—and then chain them in place to prevent their theft? Worse than that, they were the dumbest aristocrats in the history of man. They couldn't be bothered to take care of their own peasants. I mean, if you want a horse to break his back for you, do you feed him . . . or take all his hay to make yourself pillows and mattresses?

"And then on the other side you had sincere, well-meanin' folks who were even dumber than the rich. Between the anti-teckers and the no-nukers and the stop-fusion people and the small-is-beautiful types and the appropriate-technology folks and the back-to-the-landers they managed to pull the plug, to throw away the whole goddam Solar System. The car might have got us all to a gas station, running on fumes and momentum—but now that they shut the engine down there ain't enough gas left to get it started again . . .

"They let the space program die—they let all of high tech society die, because it wasn't perfect—and now the planet just hasn't got the metals or the power or the technology to bring it back; we're damn lucky to feed ourselves. Now there really *is* Only One Earth—and it never was big enough . . ."

The old man's cigarette was too short to keep smoking. He pinched it out between two fingers, salvaged the unburnt tobacco, and began to take up his tale again. Then he saw that the children were both fast asleep. He let his breath out, covered them, and blew out the candle. He thought about going downstairs to ask his son-in-law how things had gone in the fields, whether the crop had been saved . . . but the stairs were hard on the old man's our fright us, and he really did not want to risk hearing bad news just now. Instead he went to the window and watched the moon, lonely now for several decades, and after a time he cried. For the children, who could never never hope that one day their grandchildren might have the stars . . .

RUBBER SOUL

But I don't believe in this stuff, he thought, enjoying himself hugely. *I said I didn't; weren't you listening?*

He sensed amusement in those around him—Mum, Dad, Stuart, Brian, Mal and the rest—but not in response to his attempt at irony. It was more like the amusement a group of elders might feel toward a young man about to lose his virginity, amusement at his too-well-understood bravado. It was too benevolent to anger him, but it did succeed in irritating him. He determined to do this thing as well as it had ever been done.

Dead easy, he punned. *New and scary and wonderful, that's what I'm good at. Let's go!*

Then the source of the bright green light came that one increment nearer, and he was transfixed.

Oh!

Time stopped, and he began to understand.

And was grabbed by the scruff of the neck and yanked backward. Foot of the line for you, my lad! He howled his protest, but the light began to recede; he felt himself moving backward through the tunnel, slowly at first but with constant acceleration. He clutched at Dad and Mum, but for the second time they slipped through his fingers and were gone. The walls of the tunnel roared past him, the light grew faint, and then all at once he was in interstellar space, and the light was lost among a million billion other pinpoints. A planet was below him, rushing up fast, a familiar blue-green world.

Bloody hell, he thought. *Not again!*

Clouds whipped up past him. He was decelerating, somehow without stress. Landscape came up at him, an immense sprawling farm. He was aimed like a bomb at a large three-story house, but he was decelerating so sharply now that he was not afraid. Sure enough, he reached the roof at the speed of a falling leaf—and sank gracefully through the roof, and the attic, finding himself at rest just below the ceiling of a third-floor room.

Given its rural setting, the room could hardly have been more incongruous. It looked like a very good Intensive Care Unit, with a single client. Two doctors garbed in traditional white gathered around the figure on the bed, adjusting wires and tubes, monitoring terminal readouts, moving with controlled haste.

The room was high-ceilinged; he floated about six feet above the body on the bed. He had always been nearsighted. He squinted down, and recognition came with a shock.

Christ! You're joking! I done *that bit.*

He began to sink downward. He tried to resist, could not. The shaven skull came closer, enveloped him. He gave up and invested the motor centers, intending to use this unwanted body to kick and punch and scream. Too late he saw the trap: the body was full of morphine. He had time to laugh with genuine appreciation at this last joke on him, and then consciousness faded.

After a measureless time he woke. Nothing hurt; he felt wonderful and lethargic. Nonetheless he knew from experience that he was no longer drugged, at least not heavily.

Someone was standing over him, an old man he thought he knew.

"Mister Mac," he said, mildly surprised.

The other shook his head. "Nope. He's dead."

"So am I."

Another deadpan headshake from the old man. "Dirty rumor. We get 'em all the time, you and I."

His eyes widened. The voice was changed, but unmistakable. "Oh, my God—it's *you!*"

"I often wonder."

"But you're *old.*"

"So are you, son. Oh, you don't look it, I'll grant you that, but if I told you how old you are you'd laugh yourself spastic, honest. Here, let me lift your bed."

The bed raised him to a half-sitting position, deliciously comfortable. "So you froze me carcass and then brought me back to life?"

The old man nodded. "Me and him." He gestured behind him.

The light was poor, but he could make out a figure seated in darkness on the far side of the room. "Who—?"

The other stood and came forward slowly.

My God, was his first thought. *It's me!* Then he squinted—and chuckled. "What do you know? The family Jules. Hello, son."

"Hello, Dad."

"You're a man grown, I see. It's good to see you. You look good." He ran out of words.

The man addressed began to smile, and burst into tears and fled the room.

He turned back to his older visitor. "Bit of a shock, I expect."

They looked at each other for an awkward moment. There

were things that both wanted to say. Neither was quite ready yet.

"Where's Mother?" he asked finally.

"Not here," the old man said. "She didn't want any part of it."

"Really?" He was surprised, not sure whether or not to be hurt.

"She's into reincarnation, I think. This is all blasphemy and witchcraft to her. She cooperated—she gave us permission, and helped us cover up and all. But she doesn't want to hear about it. I don't know if she'll want to see you, even."

He thought about it. "I can understand that. I promised Mother once I'd never haunt her. Only fair. She still makin' music?"

"I don't think so."

There was another awkward silence.

"How's the wife?" he asked.

The old man winced slightly. "She went right back out the window a while back."

"I'm sorry."

"Sorriest thing I've seen all day, son. You comfy?"

"Yeah. How about Sean?"

"He doesn't know about this yet. His mother decided not to burden him with it while he was growing up. But you can see him if you want, in a few days. You'll like him, he's turned out well. He loves you."

A surge of happiness suffused him, settled into a warm glow. To cover it he looked around the room, squinting at the bewildering array of machines and instruments. "This must have set you back a packet."

The old man smiled for the first time. "What's the good of being a multimillionaire if you can't resurrect the dead once in a while?"

"Aye, I've thought that a few times meself." He was still not ready to speak his heart. "What about the guy that got me?"

"Copped it in the nick. Seems a lot of your best fans were behind bars."

"Why'd he do it?"

"Who knows? Some say he thought he was you, and you were an impostor. Some say he just wanted to be somebody. He said God told him to do it, 'coz you were down on churches and that."

"Oh, Jesus. The silly fucker." He thought for a time. "You know that one I wrote about bein' scared, when I was alone that time?"

"I remember."

"Truest words I ever wrote. God, what a fuckin' prophet! 'Hatred and jealousy, gonna be the death of me.' "

"You had it backward, you know."

"How do you mean?"

"Nobody ever had better reason to hate you than Jules."

He made no reply.

"And nobody ever had better reason to be jealous of you than me."

Again he was speechless.

"But it was him thought it up in time, and me pulled it off. His idea and enthusiasm. My money. Maybe nobody else on Earth could have made that much nicker drop off the books. So you got that backward, about them bein' the *death* of you." He smiled suddenly. "Old Jules. Just doin' what I told him to do, really."

"Makin' it better."

The old man nodded. "He let you under his skin, you see."

"Am I the first one they brought back, then?"

"One of the first half-dozen. That Wilson feller in California got his daughter back. It's not exactly on the National Health."

"And nobody knows but you and Jules? And Mother?"

"Three doctors. My solicitor. A cop in New York used to know, a captain, but he died. And George and Ringo know, they send their best."

He winced. "I was rough on George."

"That you were, son. He forgives you, of course. Nobody else knows in all the wide world."

"Christ, that's a relief. I thought I was due for another turn on the flaming cupcake. Can you imagine if they fuckin' *knew?* It'd be like the last time was *nothing.*"

It was the old man's first real grin, and it melted twenty years or more from his face. "Sometimes when I'm lying awake I get the giggles just thinking about it."

He laughed aloud, noting that it did not hurt to laugh. "Talk about upstaging Jesus!"

They laughed together, the old man and the middle-aged man. When the laugh ended, they discovered to their mutual surprise that they were holding hands. The irony of that struck them both simultaneously. But they were both of them used to irony that might have stunned a normal man, and used to sharing such irony with each other; they did not let go. And so now there was only the last question to be asked.

"Why did you do it, then? Spend all that money and all that time to bring me back?"

"Selfish reasons."

"Right. Did it ever occur to you that you might be calling me back from something important?"

"I reckoned that if I could pull it off, then it was okay for me to do it."

He thought wistfully of the green light . . . but he was, for better or worse, truly alive now. Which was to say that he wanted to stay alive. "Your instincts were always good. Even back in the old scufflin' days."

"I didn't much care, if you want to know the truth of it. You left me in the lurch, you know. It was the end of the dream, you dying, and everybody reckoned I was the one broke us up so it was my fault somehow. I copped it all. My music turned to shit and they stopped comin' to hear it, I don't remember which happened first. It all went sour when you snuffed it, lad. You had to go and break my balls in that last interview . . ."

"That *was* bad karma," he agreed. "Did you call me back to haunt me, then? Do you want me to go on telly and set the record straight or something?"

The grip on his hand tightened.

"I called you back because you're a better songwriter than I am. Because I miss you." The old man did not cry easily. "Because I love you." He broke, and wept unashamedly. "I've always loved you, Johnny. It's shitty without you around."

"Oh, Christ, I love you too." They embraced, clung to each other and wept together for some time.

At last the old man released him and stepped back. "It's a rotten shame we're not gay. We always did make such beautiful music together."

"Only the best fuckin' music in the history of the world."

"We will again. The others are willing. Nobody else would ever know. No tapes, nothing. Just sit around and play."

"You're incorrigible." But he was interested. "Are you serious? How could you possibly keep a thing like that secret? No bloody way—"

"It's been a *long* time," the old man interrupted. "You taught me, you taught all three of us, a long time ago, how to drop off the face of the earth. Just stop making records and giving interviews. They don't even come 'round on anniversaries anymore. It'll be dead easy."

He was feeling somewhat weary. "How . . . how long has it been?"

"Since you snuffed it? Get this—I told you it'd give you a laugh. It's been two dozen years."

He worked it out, suddenly beginning to giggle. "You mean, I'm . . . ?"

The old man was giggling too. "Yep."

He roared with laughter. "Will you still feed me, then?"

"Aye," the old man said. "And I'll always need you, too."

Slowly he sobered. The laugh had cost him the last of his strength. He felt sleep coming. "Do you really think it'll be good, old friend? Is it gonna be *fun?*"

"As much fun as whatever you've been doing for the last twenty-four years? I dunno. What was it like?"

"I dunno anymore. I can't remember. Oh—Stu was there, and Brian." His voice slurred. "I think it was okay."

"This is going to be okay, too. You'll see. I've given you the middle eight. Last verse was always your specialty."

He nodded, almost asleep now. "You always did believe in scrambled eggs."

The old man watched his sleeping friend for a time. Then he sighed deeply and went to comfort Julian and phone the others.

THE MAGNIFICENT CONSPIRACY

1.

By the time I had pulled in and put her in park, alarm bells were going off all over my subconscious so I just stayed put and looked around. After a minute and a half, I gave up. *Everything* about the place was wrong.

Even the staff. Reserved used-car salesmen are about as common as affable hangmen—but I had the whole minute and a half to myself, and as much longer as I wanted. The man semivisible through the dusty office window was clearly aware of my arrival, but he failed to get up from his chair.

So I shut off the ignition and climbed out into un-air-conditioned July, and by God even the music was wrong. It wasn't Muzak at all; it was an old Peter, Paul & Mary album. How can you psych someone into buying a clunker with music like that? Even when I began wandering around kicking tires and glancing under hoods he stayed in the office. He seemed to be reading. I was determined to get a reaction now, so I picked out the classiest car I could see (easily worth three times as much as my Dodge), hotwired her and started her up. As I'd expected, it fetched him—but he didn't hurry. Except for that, he was standard-issue salesman—which is like saying, "Except for the sun-porch, it was a standard issue fighter jet."

"Sorry, mister. That one ain't for sale."

I looked disappointed.

"Already spoken for, huh?"

"Nope. But you don't want her."

I listened to the smooth, steady rumble of the engine. "Oh, yeah? Why not? She sounds beautiful."

He nodded. "Runs beautiful, too—now. Feller sold it to us gimmicked 'er with them pellets you get from the Whitney catalog. Inside o' five hundred miles you wouldn't have no more rings than a spinster."

I let my jaw drop.

"She wouldn't even be sittin' out here, except the garage is full up. Could show you a pretty good Chev, you got your heart set on a convertible."

"Hey, listen," I broke in. "Do you realize you could've kept your mouth shut and sold me this car for two thousand flat?"

He wiped his forehead with a red handkerchief. "Yep. Couple year ago, I would've." He hitched his glasses higher on his nose and grinned suddenly. "Couple year ago I had an ulcer."

I had the same disquieting sensation you get in an earthquake when the ground refuses to behave properly. I shut the engine off. "There isn't a single sign about the wonderful bargains you've got," I complained. "The word 'honest' does not appear anywhere on your lot. You don't hurry. I've been here for three minutes and you haven't shaken my hand and you haven't tried to sell me a thing and you *don't hurry.* What the hell kind of used-car lot is this?"

He looked like he was trying hard to explain, but he only said, "Couple of year ago I had an ulcer," again, which explained nothing. I gave up and got out of the convertible. As I did so, I noticed for the first time an index card on the dashboard which read "$100."

"That can't be the price," I said flatly. "Without an *engine* she's worth more than that."

"Oh, no," he said, looking scandalized. "That ain't the price. Couldn't be: price ain't fixed."

Oh. "What determines the price?"

"The customer. What he needs, how bad he needs it, how much he's got."

This of course is classic sales-doctrine—but you're not supposed to *tell* the customer. You're supposed to go through the quaint charade of an asking price, then knock off a hastily computed amount because "I can see you're in a jam and I like your face."

"Well then," I said, trying to get this script back on the track, "maybe I'd better tell you about my situation."

"Sure," he agreed. "Come on in the office. More comfortable there. Got the air condition."

I saw him notice my purple sneakers as I got out of the convertible—which pleased me. You can't buy them that garish—you have to dye them yourself.

And halfway to the office, my subconscious identified the specific tape being played over the sound system. Just a hair too late; the song hit me before I was braced for it. I barely had time to put my legs on automatic pilot. Fortunately, the salesman was walking ahead of me, and could not see my face. *Album 1700*, side one, track six: "The Great Mandala (The Wheel of Life)."

So I told him
That he'd better
Shut his mouth
And do his job like a man
And he answered
Listen (*father didn't even come to the funeral and the face in the coffin was my own but oh God so thin and drawn like collapsed*

around the skull and the skin like gray paper and the eyes dear Jesus Christ the eyes he looked so content so hideously content *didn't he understand that he'd blown it blown it*) own it very long, Mr. Uh?"

He was standing, no, squatting by my Dodge, peering up the tailpipe. The hood was up.

If you're good enough, you can put face and mouth on automatic pilot, too. I told him I was Bob Campbell and that I had owned the Dodge for three years. I told him I was a clerk in a supermarket. I told him I had a wife and two children and an MA in Business Administration. I told him I needed a newer model car to try for a better job. It was a plausible story; he didn't seem to find anything odd about my facial expressions, and I'm sure he believed every word. By the time I had finished sketching my income and outgo, we were in the office and the door was closing on the song:

Take your place on
The Great Mandala
As it moves through your brief moment of (*click*) time that Dodge of yours had a ring job, too, Bob."

I came fully aware again, remembered my purpose.

"Ring job? Look, uh . . ." We seated ourselves.

"Arden Larsen."

"Look, Arden, that car had a complete engine overhaul not five thousand miles ago. It's—"

"Stow it, Bob. From the inside of your exhaust pipe alone my best professional estimate is that you are getting about forty or fifty miles to a quart of oil. Nobody can overhaul a slant-six that bad." I began to protest. "If that engine was even so much as steam-cleaned less'n ten thousand mile ago I'll eat my socks."

"Just a damned minute, Larsen—"

"Don't ever try to bamboozle a used-car man my age,

son—it just humiliates the both of us. Now, it's hard to tell
for sure without jackin' up the front end or drivin' her, but I'd
guess the actual value of that Dodge to be about a hundred
dollars. That's half of what it'd cost you to rent a car for as
long as the Dodge is liable to last."

"Well, of all the colossal—I don't have to listen to this
crap!" I got up and headed for the door, which was corny and
a serious mistake, because when I was halfway to the door he
hadn't said a word and when I was upon it he still hadn't said
a word and I was so puzzled at how I could have overplayed it
so badly that I actually had the door open before I remembered what lay outside it:

Tell the jailer
Not to bother
With his meal of bread and water today
He is fasting till the killing's over here and I'll get you
some ice water, Bob. Must be ninety-five in the shade out
there. You'll be okay in a minute."

"Yeah. Sure." I stumbled back to my seat and gratefully
accepted the ice water he brought from the refrigerator in a
corner of the office. I remembered to keep my back very
straight. *Get a hold on yourself, boy. It's just a song. Just some
noise—*

"Now as I was sayin', Bob—figure your car's worth a hundred. Okay. So figure the Dutchman up the road'd offer you
two hundred, and then sell it to some sorry son of a bitch for
four. Okay. Figure if you twisted his arm, he'd go three—
Mid-City Motors in town'd go that high, just to get you offa
the lot quick. Okay. So I'll give you four and a quarter."

I sprayed ice water and nearly choked. "Huh?"

"And I'll throw in that fancy convertible for three hundred, if you really want her—but you'll have to let us do the
ring job first. Won't cost you anything, and I could let you

193

have a loaner 'til we get to it. Oh yeah, an' that $100 tag you was askin' about is our best estimate of monthly gas, oil and maintenance outlay. I'd recommend a different car for a man in your situation myself, but it's up to you."

I didn't have to pretend surprise, I was flabbergasted. "Are you out of your mind?" Apparently my employer was given to understatement.

He didn't have the right set of wrinkles for a smile like that; he must have just learned how. "Feels like I get saner every day."

"But—but you can't be serious. This is a rib, right?"

Still smiling, he pulled out a wallet the size of a paperback dictionary, and counted out one hundred and twenty-five dollars in twenties and fives. He held it out in a hand so gnarled it looked like weathered maple. "What do you say? Deal?"

"I say, 'You're getting reindeer-shit all over my roof, fatso.' What's the catch?"

"No catch."

"Oh, no. You're offering me a free lunch, and I'm supposed to just fasten the bib and open my mouth, right? Is that convertible hot, or what?"

He sighed, scratched behind his glasses. "Bob, your attitude makes sense, in a world like this. That's why I don't much like a world like this, and that's why I'm working here. Now I understand how you feel. I've seen ten dozen variations of the same reaction since I started working for Mr. Cardwell, and it makes me a little sadder every time. That convertible ain't hot and there ain't no other catch neither. I'm offerin' you the car for what she's honestly worth, and if you can't believe that, why, you just go down the line and see the Dutchman. He'll skin you alive, but he won't upset you any."

I know when people are angry at me. He was angry, but not at me. So I probed. "Larsen, you've got to be completely crazy."

He blew up.

"You're damn right I am! Crazy means out o' step with the world, and accordin' to the rules o' the world, I'm supposed to cheat you out of every dime I smell on ya plus ten percent an' if you like that world so much that you wanna subsidize it then you get yer ass outa here an' go see the Dutchman but *whatever* you do *don't* you tell him we sent ya you got that?"

Nothing in the world makes a voice as harsh as the shortness of breath caused by a run-on sentence. I waited until he had fed his starving lungs and then said, "I want to see the manager," and he emptied them again very slowly and evenly, so that when he closed his eyes I knew he was close to hyperventilating. He clenched his fingers on the desk between us as though he were trying to pull it toward him, and when he opened his eyes the anger was gone from them.

"Okay, Bob. Maybe Mr. Cardwell can explain it to you. I ain't got the right words."

I nodded and got up.

"Bob . . ." He was embarrassed now. "I didn't have no call to bark at you thataway. I can't blame you for bein' suspicious. Sometimes I miss my ulcers myself. It's—well, it's a lot easier to live in a world of mud if you tell yourself there ain't no such thing as dry land."

It was the first sensible thing he'd said.

"What I mean, I'm sorry."

"Thanks for the ice water," I said.

He relaxed and smiled again. "Mr. Cardwell's in the garage out back. You take it easy in that heat."

I knew that I'd stalled long enough for the cassette or record or whatever it was to have ended, but I treated the doorknob like an angry rattlesnake just the same. But when I opened it, the only thing that hit me in the face was the hot dry air I'd expected. I left.

2.

I went through an arched gate in the plank fence that abutted the office's rear wall, and followed a wide strip of blacktop through weedy flats to the garage.

It was a four-bay job, a big windowless wood building surrounded with the usual clutter of handtrucks, engine blocks, transmissions, gas cans, fenders, drive trains, and rusted oil drums. All four bays were closed, in spite of the heat. It was set back about five hundred yards from the office, and the field behind it was lushly overgrown with dead cars, a classic White Elephant's Graveyard that seemed better tended than most. As I got closer I realized the field was actually organized: a section for GM products, one for Chryslers, one for Fords and so on, each marked with a sign and subdivided by model and, apparently, year. A huge Massey-Ferguson sat by one of three access roads, ready to haul the next clunker in to its appointed resting place. There was big money in this operation, very impressive money, and I just couldn't square that with Arden Larsen's crackpot pricing policy.

Arden seemed to have flipped the cassette to side two of *Album 1700.* I passed beneath a speaker that said it dug rock and roll music, and entered the garage through a door to the right of the four closed bays. Inside, I stopped short. Whoever heard of an air- conditioned garage? Especially one this size.

Big money.

Over on the far side of the room, just in front of a Rambler, the floor grew a man, like the Wicked Witch melting in reverse. It startled the hell out of me—until I realized he had only climbed out of one of those rectangular pits the better garages have for jobs where a lift might get in the way. With the help of unusually efficient lighting, I studied him as he approached me.

Late fifties, snow white hair and goatee, strong jaw and incongruously soft mouth. A big man, reminding me strongly of Burl Ives, but less bulky, whipcord fit. An impression of enormous energy, but used only by volition—he walked slowly, clearly because he saw no need to hurry. Paradoxical hands: thin-fingered and aristocratic, but with the ground-in grime which is the unmistakable trademark of the professional or dedicated-amateur mechanic. The right one held a pipe-wrench. His overalls were oily and torn, but he wore them like a not-rented tux.

I absorbed and stored all these details automatically, however, while most of my attention was taken up by the utter *peacefulness* of his face, of his eyes, of his expression and carriage and manner. I had never seen a man so manifestly content with his lot. It showed in the purely decorative way in which the wrinkles of his years lay upon his face; it showed in the easy swing of his big shoulders and the purposeful but carefree stride; it showed in the eager yet unhurried way that his eyes measured me: not as a cat sizes up another cat, but as a happy baby investigates a new person—with delighted interest. My purple sneakers *pleased* him. He was plainly a man who drank of his life with an unquenchable thirst, and it annoyed the hell out of me, because I knew good and goddam well when was the last time I had seen a man possessed of such peace and because nothing on earth was going to make me consciously acknowledge it.

But I am not a man whose emotions are wired into his control circuits. I smiled as he neared, and my body language said I was confused, but amiably so.

"Mr. Cardwell?"

"That's right. What can I do for you?" The way he asked it, it was not a conversational convention.

"My name's Bob Campbell. I—uh . . ."

His eyes twinkled. "Of course. You want to know if Arden's crazy, or me, or the both of us." His lips smiled, then got pried apart by his teeth into a full-blown grin.

"Well—something like that. He offered to buy my car for, uh, more than it's worth, and then he offered to sell me the classiest-looking car on the lot for . . ."

"Mr. Campbell, I'll stand behind whatever prices Arden made you."

"But you don't know what they are yet."

"I don't need to," he said, still grinning. "I know Arden."

"But he offered to do a free ring job on the car, for Chrissake."

"Oh, that convertible. Mr. Campbell, he didn't do that 'for Chrissake'—Arden's not a church-going man. He did it for his sake, and for mine and for yours. That car isn't worth a thing without that ring job—the aggravation it'd give you would use up more energy than walking."

"But—but," I sputtered, "how can you possibly survive doing that kind of business?"

His grin disappeared. "How long can any of us survive, Mr. Campbell, doing business any other way? I sell cars for what I believe them to be genuinely worth, and I pay much more than that for them so that people will sell them to me. What's wrong with that?"

"But how can you make a profit?"

"I can't."

I was shocked speechless. When he saw this, Cardwell smiled again—but this time it was a smile underlain with sadness. "Money, young man, is a symbol representing the life energy of those who subscribe to it. It is a useful and even necessary symbol—but because it is only a symbol, it is possible to amass on paper more profit than there actually is to be made. The more people who insist on making a profit, all the time, in every dealing, the more people who will be required to go bankrupt—to pour their life-energy into the system and get nothing back—in order to keep the machine running. A profit is without honor, save in its own country—there is certainly nothing sacred about one. Especially if you don't need it."

I continued to gape.

"Perhaps I should explain," he went on, "that I was born with a golden spoon in my mouth. My family has been unspeakably wealthy for twelve generations, controlling one of the oldest and most respected fortunes in existence—the kind that calls for battalions of tax lawyers in every country in the world. My personal worth is so absurdly enormous that if I were to set a hundred dollar bill on fire every minute of my waking life I would never succeed in getting out of the highest income tax bracket."

"You . . ." My system flooded with adrenalin. "You *can't* be *that* Cardwell."

BIG money.

"There are times when I almost wish I wasn't. But since I have no choice at all in the matter, I'm trying to make the best of it."

"By throwing money away?" I yelped, and fought for control.

"No. By putting it back where it belongs. I inherited control of a stupendous age-old leech—and I'm forcing it to regurgitate."

"I don't understand." I shook my head vigorously and

rubbed a temple with my thumb. "I just don't understand."

He smiled the sad smile again, and the pipe-wrench loosened in his grip for the first time. "You don't have to, you know. You can take your money from Arden and drive home in a loaner and pick up your convertible in a few days and then put it all out of your mind. All I'm selling is used cars."

He was asking me a question.

I shook my head again, more slowly. "No—no, I'd like to understand, I think. Will you explain?"

He put the wrench down on an oil drum. "Let's sit down."

There were a pair of splendidly comfortable chairs in the rear of the garage, with foldaway armrests that let you select for comfort or elbow room at need. Beyond them stood an expensive (but not frost-free) refrigerator, from which Cardwell produced two frosty bottles of Dos Equis. I accepted one and sat in the nearer chair. Cardwell sprawled back in his and put his feet up on a beheaded slant six engine, and when he drank he gave the beer his full attention.

I regret to say I did not. *Despite* all the evidence, I could not make myself believe that this grease-stained mechanic with his sneakers on an engine block was actually *the* Raymond Sinclair Cardwell. If it was true, my fee was going to quintuple, and Hakluyt was fucking well going to pay it. Send a man after a cat, and forget to mention that it's a black panther—*Jesus*.

Cardwell's chair had a beverage-holder built into the armrest; he set his beer in it and folded his arms easily. He spoke slowly, thoughtfully; and he had that knack of observing you as he spoke, modifying his word-choice by feedback. I have the knack myself; but I wondered why a man in his situation would have troubled to acquire it. I found myself trying as hard to understand him as he was trying to be understood.

The Magnificent Conspiracy

★ ★ ★ ★ ★

I don't know (he said) if I can convey what it's like to be born preposterously wealthy, Mr. Campbell, so I won't try. It presents one with an incredible view of reality that cannot be imagined by a normal human being. The world of the very rich is only tangentially connected with the real world, for all that their destinies are intertwined. I lived totally in that other world and that world-view for thirty-six years, happily moving around mountains of money with a golden bulldozer, stoking the fires of progress. I rather feel I was a typical multibillionaire, if that conveys anything to you. My only eccentricity was a passion for working on cars, which I had absorbed in my youth from a chauffeur I admired. I had access to the finest assistance and education the world had to offer, and became rather handy. As good as I was with international finance and real estate and arbitrage and interlocking cartels and all the other avenues through which a really enormous fortune is interconnected with the world. I enjoyed manipulating my fortune, *using* it—in some obscure way I believe I felt a duty to do so. And I *always* made a profit.

It was in London that it changed.

I had gone there to personally oversee a large and complex merger involving seven nations. The limousine had just left the airport when the first shot killed my driver. He was the man who taught me how to align-bore an engine block and his name was Ted. The window was down; he just hurled sideways and soiled his pants. I think I figured it out as the second shot got my personal bodyguard, but by then we were under the wheels of the semi. I woke up eight weeks later, and one of the first things I learned is that no one is ever truly unconscious. I woke up speaking in a soft but pronounced British accent precisely like that of my private nurses, and it persisted for two days.

I discovered that Phillip, the bodyguard, had died. So had Lisa, a lady who meant entirely too little to me. So had Teal, the London regional director who had met my plane, and the driver of the semi. The rifleman had been apprehended: a common laborer, driven mad by his poverty. He had taken a gun to traffic in the same way that a consistently mistreated Doberman will attack anyone who approaches, because it seemed to him the only honorable and proper response to the world.

Cardwell drank deep from his beer.

My convalescence was long. The physical crisis was severe, but the spiritual trauma was infinitely greater. Like Saint Paul, I had been smashed from my horse, changed at once from a mover and shaper to a terrified man who hurt terribly in many places. The best drugs in the world cannot truly kill pain—they blunt its edge without removing it, or its terrible reminder of mortality. I had nearly died, and I suddenly had a tremendous need to explain to myself why that would have been such a tragedy. I could not but wonder who would have mourned for me, and how much, and I had a partial answer in the shallow extent of my own mourning for Ted and Phillip and Teal and Lisa. The world I had lived my life in was one in which there was little love, in which the glue of social relationships was not feelings, but common interests. I had narrowly, by the most costly of medical miracles, avoided inconveniencing many hundreds of people, and not a damn thing else.

And, of course, I could not deal with this consciously or otherwise. My world-view lacked the "spiritual vocabulary" with which to frame these concepts: I desperately needed to resolve a conflict I could not even express. It delayed my effective recovery for weeks beyond the time when I was technically "on my feet"—I was simply unable to reenter the lists of life, unable to see why living was worth the terrible danger of dying. And so my body healed slowly, by the same instinctive wisdom with which it had kept my forebrain in a coma until it could cope with the extent of my injuries.

And then I met John Smiley.

Cardwell paused for so long that I had begun to search for a prompting remark when he continued.

John was an institution at that hospital. He had been there longer than any of the staff or patients. He had not left the bed he was in for twelve years. Between his ribcage and his knees he was mostly plastic bags and tubes and things that are to a colostomy bag what a Rolls-Royce is to a dogcart. He needed one and sometimes two operations every year, and his refusal to die was an insult to medical science, and he was the happiest man I have ever met in my life.

My life had taught me all the nuances of pleasure; joy, however, was something I had only dimly sensed in occasional others and failed to really recognize. Being presented with a pure distillate of the thing forced me to learn what it was—and from there it was only a short step to realizing that I lacked it. You only begin to perceive where you itch when you learn how to scratch.

John Smiley received the best imaginable care, far better than he was entitled to. His only financial asset was an insurance company which grudgingly disbursed enough to keep him alive, but he got the kind of service and personal attention usually given only to a man of my wealth. This puzzled me greatly when I first got to know him, the more so when I learned that he could not explain it himself. But I soon understood.

Virtually every doctor, nurse, and long-term patient in the hospital worshipped him. The rare, sad few who would have blackly hated him were identified by the rest and kept from him. The more common ones who desperately needed to meet him were also identified, and sent *to* him, subtly or directly as indicated.

Mr. Campbell, John Smiley was simply a fountain of the human spirit, a healer of souls. Utterly wrecked in body, his whole life telescoped down to a bed he didn't rate and a TV he couldn't afford and the books scrounged for him by nurses and interns and the Pall Malls that appeared magically on his bedside table every morning—and the people who chanced to come through his door—John made of life a magnificent thing. He listened to the social and sexual and financial and emotional woes of anyone who came into his room, drawing their troubles out of them with his great gray eyes, and he sent them away lighter in their hearts, with a share of the immeasurable joy he had somehow found within himself. He had helped the charge nurse when her marriage failed, and he had helped the head custodian find the strength to raise his mongoloid son alone, and he had helped the director of the hospital to kick Demerol. And while I knew him, he helped a girl of eighteen die with grace and dignity. In that hospital, they sent the tough ones around, on one pretext or another, to see John Smiley—and that was simply all it took.

He had worked for the police as a plainclothesman, and one day as he and his partner were driving his own car into the police garage, a two-ton door had given way and come down on them. Ackroyd, his partner, had been killed outright, and so Mrs. Ackroyd received an award equivalent to half a million dollars. John's wife was less fortunate—his life was saved. They explained to her that under the law she would not collect a cent until he was dead. Then they added softly that they gave him a month at the outside. Twelve years later he was still chain-smoking Pall Malls and bantering with his wife's boy-friend when they came to visit him, which was frequently.

I wandered into John Smiley's room one day, sick in my heart and desperately thirsty for something more than thirty-six years had taught me of life, seeking for a reason to go on living. Like many others before and since, I drank from John Smiley, drank from his seemingly inexhaustible well of joy in living—and in the process, I acquired the taste.

I learned some things.

Mostly, I think, I learned the difference between pleasure and joy. I suppose I had already made the distinction, subcon-sciously, but I considered the latter a fraud, an illusion over-laid upon the former to lend it respectability. John Smiley proved me wrong. His pleasures were as restricted as mine had been unrestricted—and his joy was so incandescently superior to mine that on the night of the day I met him I found myself humming the last verse of "Richard Corey" in my mind.

Cardwell paused, and his voice softened.

He forgave me my ignorance.

He forgave me my money and my outlook and my arro-gance and *treated me as an equal,* and most amazing of all, he made me forgive myself.

The word "forgive" is interesting. Someone robs you of your wallet, and they find him down the line and bring him back to you, saying, "We found your wallet on this man," and you say, "That's all right. He can have—can have had—it; I fore-give it to him."

To preserve his sanity, John Smiley had been forced to "fore-give" virtually everything God had given him. In his presence you could not do less yourself.

And so I even gave up mourning a "lost innocence" I had never had, and put the shame he inspired in me to positive use. I began designing my ethics.

I interrupted for the first and last time.

"A rich man who would design his own ethics is a dangerous thing," I said.

Damn right (he said, with the delight of one who sees that his friend really *understands*). A profit is without honor except in its own country—but that's a hell of a lot of territory. The economic system reacts, with the full power of the racial unconscious, to preserve itself—and I had no wish to tilt at the windmill.

I confess that my first thought was of simply giving my money away, in a stupendous orgy of charity, and taking a job in a garage. But John was wise enough to be able to show me that that would have been as practical as disposing of a warehouse full of high explosive by setting fire to it with a match. You may have read in newspapers, some years back, of a young man who attempted to give away an inheritance, a *much* smaller fortune than mine. He is now hopelessly insane, shattered by the power that was thrust upon him. *He did not do it to himself.*

So I started small, and very slowly. The first thing I did was to heal the ulcers of the hospital's accounting department. They had been juggling desperately to cover the cost of the care that John Smiley was getting, so I bought the hospital and told them to juggle away, whenever they felt they should. That habit was hard to break; I bought forty-seven hospitals in the next two years, and quietly instructed them to run whatever loss they had to, to provide maximum care and comfort for their patients. I spent the next six years working in them, a month or two each, as a janitor. This helped me to assess their management, replacing entire staffs down to the bedpan level when necessary. It also added considerably to my education. There are many hospitals in the world, Mr. Campbell, some good, some bad, but I know for certain that forty-seven of them are wonderful places in which to hurt.

The janitor habit was hard to break, too. Over the next ten years I toured my empire, like a king traveling incognito to learn the *flavor* of his land. I held many and varied jobs, for my empire is an octopus, but they all amounted to janitor. I spent ten years toiling anonymously at the very borders of my fortune, at the last interface between it and the people it involved, the communities it affected. And without me at the helm, for *ten years,* the nature and operation of my fortune changed in no way whatsoever, and when I realized that it shook me. I gave up my tour of inspection and went to my estate in British Columbia and holed up for a few years, thinking it through. Then I began effecting changes. This used-car lot is only one of them. It's my favorite, though, so it's the first one I've implemented and it's where I choose to spend my personal working hours.

But there are many other changes planned.

3.

The silence stretched like a spring, but when at last I spoke my voice was soft, quiet, casual, quite calm. "And you expect me to believe that none of these changes will make a profit?" He blinked and started, precisely as if a tape recorder had started talking back to him.

"My dear Mr. Campbell," he said with a trace of sadness, "I frankly don't expect you to believe a word I've said."

My voice was still calm. "Then why tell me all this?"

"I'm not at all sure. But I believe it has much to do with the fact that you are the first person to *ask* me about it since I opened this shop."

Calm gone. "Bullshit," I roared, much too loud. "Bullfuckingshit, I mean a king-size meadow-muffin! Do you goddammit," I was nearly incoherent, "think I was fucking born yesterday? Sell *me* a free lunch? You simple sonofabitch I *am not that stupid!*"

This silence did not stretch; it lay there like a bludgeoned dove. I wondered whether all garages echoed like this and I'd never noticed. *The hell with control, I don't need control, control is garbage, it's just me and him.* My spine was very straight.

"I'm sorry," he said at last, as sorrowfully as though my anger were truly his fault. "I humbly apologize, Mr. Campbell. I took you for a different kind of man. But I can see now that you're no fool."

His voice was infinitely sad.

"I don't mind a con, but this is stupid. You're giving away cars and you and Larsen are plenty to handle the traffic. I'm your only customer—what do you take me for?"

"The first wave has passed," he said. "There are only so many fools in any community, only a few naive or desperate enough to turn out for a free lunch. It was quite busy here for six months or so, but now all the fools have been accommodated. It will be weeks, months, before word-of-mouth gets around, before people learn that the cars I've sold them are good cars, that my guarantees are genuine. Dozens will have to return, scream for service, promptly receive it and numbly wander home before the news begins to spread. It will get quite busy again then, for a while, and probably very noisy, too—but at the moment I'm not even a Silly Season filler in the local paper. The editor killed it, as any good editor would. He's no fool, either.

"I'm recruiting fools, Mr. Campbell. There was bound to be a lull after the first wave hit. But I believe that the second will be a tsunami."

My voice was a whip. "And this is how you're going to save the world? By doing lube jobs and fixing mufflers?"

"This is one of the ways, yes. It's not surgery, but it should help comfort the patient until surgery can be undertaken. It's hard to concentrate on anything when you have a boil on your ass."

"What?"

"Sorry. A metaphor I borrowed from John Smiley, at the same time I borrowed the idea itself. 'Ray,' he said to me, 'you're talking about using your money to make folks more comfortable, to remove some of the pointless distractions so they have the energy to sit down and think. Well, the one boil on everybody's ass is his vehicle—everybody that has to have one, which is most everybody.' Everywhere I went over the next decade, I heard people bitterly complaining about their cars, pouring energy and money into them, losing jobs because of them, going broke because of them, being killed because of them. So I'm lancing the boil—in this area anyway.

"It makes an excellent test-operation, too. If people object too strongly to having their boils lanced, then I'll have to be *extremely* circumspect in approaching their cancers. Time will tell."

"And no one's tried to stop you from giving away cars?"

"I don't give away cars. I sell them at a fair price. But the effect is similar, and yes, there have been several attempts to stop me by various legal means. But there has never been a year of my life when I was being sued for less than a million dollars.

"Then there were the illegal attempts. For a while this lot was heavily, and unobtrusively, guarded, and twice those guards found it necessary to break a few arms. I've dismissed them all for the duration of the lull between waves, but there'll be an army here if and when I need it.

"But until the next wave of customers hits, the only violence I'm expecting is a contract assassination or two."

"Oh?"

The anger drained from my voice as professional control switched in again. I noted that his right hand was out of sight behind his chair—on the side I had not yet seen. I sat bolt upright.

"Yes, the first one is due any time now. He'll probably show up with a plausible identity and an excellent cover-story, and he'll probably demand to see the manager on the obvious pretext. He'll wear strikingly gaudy shoes to draw the attention of casual witnesses from his face, and his shirt will have a high collar, and he'll hold his spine very straight. He'll be completely untraceable, expensive, and probably good at his work, but his employers will almost certainly have kept him largely in the dark, and so he'll underestimate his opposition until it is too late. Only then will he realize that I could have come out of that pit with an M-16 as easily as with a pipe wrench if the situation had seemed to warrant it. What *is* that thing, anyway? It's too slim for a blow-gun."

If you've lost any other hope of misdirecting the enemy, try candor. I sighed, relaxed my features in a gesture of surrender, and very slowly reached up and over my shoulder. Gripping the handle that nestled against my last few vertebrae, I pulled straight up and out, watching the muscles of his right arm tense where they disappeared behind the chair and wishing mightily that I knew what his hand was doing. I pointedly held the weapon in a virtually useless overhand grip, but I was unsettled to see him pick up on that—he was altogether too alert for my taste. *Hang on, dammit, you can still pull this off if you just hang on.*

"Stiffened piano wire," I said, meeting his eyes, "embedded in a hardwood grip and filed sharp. You put it between the correct two ribs and shove. Ruptures the heart, and the pericardial sac self-seals on the way out. Pressure builds. If you do it properly, the victim himself thinks it's a heart attack, and the entry wound is virtually undetectable. A full-scale autopsy would pick it up—but when an overweight car dealer in his fifties has a heart attack, pathologists don't generally get up on their toes."

"Unless he happens to be a multibillionaire," Cardwell noted.

"My employers will regret leaving me in ignorance. Fluoroscope in the fence gate?"

"The same kind they use in airports. If that weapon hadn't been so damned interesting, you'd never have reached the garage."

"I wanted to do the research, but they were paying double for a rush job." I sighed. "I knew better. Or should have. Now what?"

"Now let go of that thing and kick it far away."

I did so at once.

"Now you can have another beer and tell me some things."

"Sorry, Cardwell. No names. They sent me in blind, and I'll speak to them about that one day, but I don't give names. It's bad for business. Go ahead and call the man."

"You misunderstand me, sir. I already know Hakluyt's name quite well, and I have no intention of calling police of any description."

I knew the location of every scrap of cover for twenty yards in any direction, and I favored the welding tanks behind me and to my left—he looked alert enough not to shoot at them at such close range, and they were on wheels facing him. If I could tip my chair backwards and come at him from behind the tank—

"—and I'd rather not kill you unless you force me to, so please unbunch those muscles."

There was no way he was going to let me walk away from this, and there was no way I was going to sit there and let him pot me at his leisure, so there was no question of sitting still, and so no one was more surprised than me when the muscles of my calves and thighs unbunched and I sat still.

Perhaps I believed him.

"Ask your questions," I said.

"Why did you take this job?"

I broke up. "Oh, my God," I whooped, "how did a nice girl like me wind up in such a profession, you mean?" The ancient gag was suddenly very hilarious, and I roared with laughter as I gave the punchline. "Just lucky, I guess."

Pure tension-release, of course. But damned if he didn't laugh at the old chestnut, too—or at himself for all I know. We laughed together until I was done, and then he said, "But why?" and I sobered up.

"For the money, of course."

He shook his head. "I don't believe you."

What's in your right hand, old man? I only shrugged. "It's the truth."

He shook his head again. "Some of your colleagues, perhaps. But I watched your face while I told you my story, and *your* empathic faculty seems to be functioning quite nicely. You're personally involved in this, involved with me. You're too damn mad at me, and it's confusing you as you sit there, spoiling your judgment. Oh no, son, you can't fool me.

You're *some* kind of idealist. But *what brand?*"

There isn't a policeman in the world who knows my name, none of my hits have so much as come to the attention of Homicide, and the reason for it is that my control is flawless, I am an unflappable killing machine, like I said, my emotions aren't even in circuit, and well yes, I had gotten hot under the collar a couple of times this afternoon for reasons I would certainly think about when I got a chance, but now of course it was killing floor time and I was in total command, and so I was again surprised and shocked to find myself springing up from my chair and, not diving behind the welding tanks, or even leaping for his right hand, but simply running flat out full tilt in plain sight for the door.

It was the most foolish imaginable move and half of my mind screamed, *Fool! Fool! At least run broken field your back is a fucking perfect target you'll never get halfway to the door* with every step until I was halfway to the door and then it shut up until I had reached the door and then the other half said quietly *I knew he wouldn't shoot* but then I had the door open and both halves screamed. It hadn't occurred to any of us that the sound system might be antiquated enough to use those miserable eight-track tapes.

Eight-tracks break down frequently, they provide mediocre sound quality under the best playback, their four-program format often leaves as much as ten minutes of dead air between programs, and you can't rewind or cue them. And they don't shut themselves off when they're done. They repeat indefinitely.

Hunger stopped him
He lies still in his cell
Death has gagged his accusations
We are free now

We can kill now
We can hate now
Now we can end the world
We're not guilty
He was crazy
And it's been going on for ten thousand years!

It is possible for an unrestrained man to kill himself with his hands. I moved to do so, and Cardwell hit me from behind like a bag of cement. One wrist broke as I landed, and he grabbed the other. He shouted things at me, but not loud enough to be heard over the final chorus:

Take your place on the Great Mandala
As it moves through your brief moment of time
Win or lose now: you must choose now
And if you lose you've only wasted your (*life* is *what it really was even if they called it five years he never came out the front door again so it was life imprisonment, right? and maybe the Cong would've killed him just as dead but they wouldn't have raped him first and they wouldn't have starved him not literally we could have been heroes together if only he hadn't been a fucking coward coward coward . . .*)

"Who was a coward?" Caldwell asked distantly, and I took it the wrong way and screamed, "*Him!* Not me! HIM!" and then I realized that the song had ended and it was very very silent out, only the distant murmuring of highway traffic and the power-hum from the speakers and the echo of my words; and I thought about what I had just said, and seven years' worth of the best rationalizations I ever built came thundering down around my ears. The largest chunk came down on my skull and smashed it flat.

Gil, I'm sorry!

4.

Ever since Nam I've been accustomed to coming awake instantly—sometimes with a weapon in my hand. I had forgotten what a luxurious pleasure it can be to let awareness and alertness seep back in at their own pace, to be truly *relaxed*. I lay still for some time, aware of my surroundings only in terms of their peacefulness, before it occurred to me to identify them. Nor did I feel, then, the slightest surprise or alarm at the defection of my subconscious sentries. It was as though in some back corner of my mind a dozen yammering voices had, for the first time within memory, shut up. All decisions were made—

I was in the same chair I'd left so hastily. It was tilted and reshaped into something more closely resembling the acceleration cradles astronauts take off in, only more comfortable. My left wrist was set and efficiently splinted, and hurt surprisingly little. Above me girders played geometric games across the high curved ceiling, interspersed with diffused-light fixtures that did not hurt to look at. Somewhere to my left, work was being done. It produced sound, but sound is divided into music and noise and somehow this clattering wasn't noise. I waited until it stopped, with infinite patience, in no hurry at all.

When there had been no sound for a while I got up and turned and saw Cardwell again emerging from the pit beneath the Rambler, with a thick streak of grease across his forehead and a skinned knuckle. He beamed. "I love ball joints. Your wrist okay?"

"Yes, thanks."

He came over, turned my chair back into a chair, and sank

215

into his own. He produced cigarettes and gave me one. I noticed a wooden stool, obviously handmade, lying crippled near a workbench. I realized that Cardwell had sawed off and split two of its legs to make the splints on my wrist. The stool was quite old, and all at once I felt more guilt and shame for its destruction than I did for having come to murder its owner. This amused me sourly. I took my cigarette to the front of the garage, where one of the great bay doors now stood open, and watched night sky and listened to crickets and bull frogs while I smoked. Shop closed, Arden gone home. After a while Cardwell got up and came to the door, too, and we stepped out into the darkness. The traffic, too, had mostly gone home for the night, and there was no moon. The dark suited me fine.

"My name," I said softly, "is Bill Maeder."

From out of the black Cardwell's voice was serene. "Pleased to meet you," was all he said.

We walked on.

"I used to be a twin," I said, flicking the cigarette butt beneath my walking feet. "My brother's name was Gil, and we were identical twins. After enough people have called your twin your Other Half, you begin to believe it. I guess we allowed ourselves to become polarized, because that suited everyone's sense of symmetry or some damned thing. Yin and Yang Maeder, they called us. All our lives we disagreed on everything, and we loved each other deeply.

"Then they called us in for our draft physical. I showed up and he didn't and so they sent me to Nam and Gil to Leavenworth. I walked through the jungles and came out a hero. Gil died in his cell at the end of a protracted hunger strike. A man who is starving to death smells like fresh-baked bread, did you know that? I spent my whole first furlough practically living in his cell, arguing with him and screaming at him, and he just sat there the whole time smelling like whole wheat right out of the oven."

Cardwell said nothing. For a while we kept strolling. Then I stopped in my tracks and said, "For seven years I told myself that *he* was the coward, that he was the chump, that he had failed the final test of survival. My father is a drunk now. My mother is a Guru Maharaj Ji premie." I started walking again, and still Cardwell was silent. "I was the coward, of course. Rather than admit I was wrong to let them make me into a killer, I gloried in it. I went freelance." We had reached my Dodge, and I stopped for the last time by the passenger-side door. "Goodness, sharing, caring about other people, ethics and morals and all that—as long as I believed that they were just a shuck, lies to keep the sheep in line, I could function, my choice made sense. If there is no such thing as hope, despair can be no sin. If there is no truth, one lie is no worse than another. Come to think of it, your Arden said something like that." I sighed. "But I hated that God damned Mandala song, the one about the draft resister who dies in jail. It came out just before I was shipped out to Nam." I reached through the open car window and took the Magnum from the glove compartment. "Right after the funeral." I put the barrel between my teeth and aimed for the roof of my mouth.

Cardwell was near, but he stood stock-still. All he said was, "Some people never learn."

My finger paused on the trigger.

"Gil will be glad to see you. You two tragic expiators will get on just fine. While the rest of us clean up the mess you left behind you. Go ahead. We'll manage."

I let my hand fall. "What are you talking about?"

All at once he was blazing mad, and a multibillionaire's rage is a terrible thing to behold. "You simple egocentric bastard, did it ever occur to you that you might be *needed?*

That the brains and skills and talent you've been using to kill strangers, to play head-games with yourself, are scarce resources? Trust an assassin to be arrogant; you colossal jackass, *do you think Arden Larsens grow on trees?* A man in my kind of business can't recruit through the want ads. But I need people with *guts.*"

"To do what?" I said, and threw the pistol into the darkness.